THAT WICKED HARLOT

Cover Design and Interior Format

Georgette BROWN

THAT WICKED HARLOT

FREE BOOK

You won't believe what this rakish
nobleman proposes for a wager!

Get your FREE copy of An Indecent Wager at:

http://dl.bookfunnel.com/62lpwgvwxh

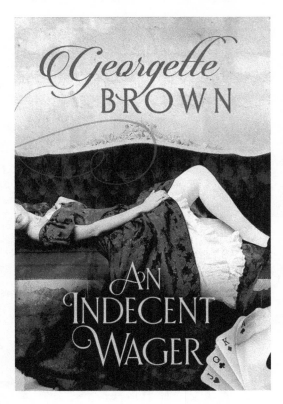

CHAPTER ONE

(

THE BEAUTIFUL WOMAN WRAPPED IN the arms of Radcliff M. Barrington, the fourth Baron Broadmoor, sighed into a wide smile as she nestled her body between his nakedness and the bed sheets. Gazing down at Lady Penelope Robbins, his mistress of nearly a twelvemonth, Broadmoor allowed her a moment to indulge in the afterglow of her third orgasm though he had yet to satisfy his own hardened arousal. He brushed his lips against her brow and happened to glance toward the corner of her bed chamber, where a man's waistcoat was draped over the back of a chair. He did not recognize it as his own. The fineness of the garment suggested that neither did it belong to one of her male servants.

Penelope was entertaining another lover, he concluded even as she murmured compliments regarding his skills as a lover. The realization came as no surprise to him. Indeed, he had suspected for some time. What surprised him was that he cared not overmuch. Nor had he the faintest curiosity as to who her other lover might be. He wondered, idly rather than seriously, why he continued to seek her company. Or she his. They had very little in common. He knew that from the start and yet had allowed her to seduce him into her bed.

He was possessed of enough breeding, wealth, and countenance to be able to command any number of women as his mistress. With black hair that waved above an ample brow and softened the square lines of his jaw, charcoal eyes that sparkled despite the dark hue, and an impeccable posture that made him taller than most of his peers, Broadmoor presented an impressive appearance. He had no shortage of women setting their caps at him. A number of his friends kept dancers or opera singers, but he had never been partial to breaking the hearts of those young things. In contrast, Penelope was a seasoned widow and had little expectation of him, having been married once before to a wealthy but vastly older baronet, and scorning a return to that institution, preferred instead to indulge in the freedoms of widowhood.

Pulling the sheets off her, he decided it was his turn to spend. She purred her approval when he covered her slender body with his muscular one. Angling his hips, he prepared to thrust himself into her when a shrill and familiar voice pierced his ears.

"I care not that he is indisposed! If the Baron is here, I *will* speak to him!"

The voice was imperial. Haughty. Broadmoor recognized it in an instant.

Penelope's eyes flew open. "Surely that is not your aunt I hear?"

His aunt, Lady Anne Barrington, was not wont to visit him in his own home at Grosvenor Square, let alone that of his mistress. He knew Anne found him cold, heartless, and arrogant. He had a dreadful habit of refusing to encourage her histrionics, and in the role of the indulgent nephew, he was a miserable failure.

"Let us pretend we do not hear her," Penelope added, wrapping her arms about him.

It would be easier to silence a skewered pig, Broadmoor thought to himself.

A timid but anxious knock sounded at the door.

"What is it?" Penelope snapped at the maid who entered and apologized profusely for the interruption, informing them that a most insistent woman waited in the drawing room and had threatened, if she was not attended to with the utmost haste, to take herself up the stairs in search of his lordship herself.

"I fear there is no immediate escape," Broadmoor said, kissing the frown on his mistress' brow before donning his shirt and pants and wrapping a robe about himself. "But I shall return."

Before descending the stairs, he took a moment for his arousal to settle.

Whatever had compelled his aunt to come to the home of his mistress had better be of damned importance.

"Anne. To what do I owe this unexpected visit?" he asked of his uncle's wife when he strode into the room.

He discerned Anne to be in quite a state of disconcertion for she only sported two long strands of pearls—far fewer than the five or so he was accustomed to seeing upon her. Her pale pink gown did not suit her complexion and made her pallor all the more grey in his eyes.

"Radcliff! Praise the heavens I have found you!" she cried upon seeing him.

He refrained from raising an inquisitive brow. Undaunted by the lack of response from her nephew, Anne continued, "We are *undone*, Radcliff! Undone! Ruined!"

His first thought was of her daughter, Juliana, who recently had had her come-out last Season. Had the girl run off to Gretna Green with some irascible young blood? He would not hesitate to give chase, but Juliana had always impressed him as a sensible young woman with an agreeable disposition—despite whom she had for a mother.

"I can scarce breathe with the thought!" Anne bemoaned. "And you know my nerves to be fragile! Oh, the treachery of it all!"

She began to pace the room while furiously waving the fan she clutched in her hand.

"I could never show my face after this," she continued. "How fortunate your uncle is not alive to bear witness to the most disgraceful ruin ever to befall a Barrington! Though I would that he had not left me to bear the burden all alone. The strain that has been put upon me—who else, I ask, has had to suffer not only the loss of her husband and now this—this unspeakable *disgrace*? I have no wish to speak ill of your uncle, but now I think it selfish of him to have gone off to the Continent with Wellington when he *knew* he would be put in harm's way. And for what end? What end?"

Broadmoor did not reveal his suspicions that his uncle had taken himself to the Continent as much as a means to relieve himself from being hen-pecked by his wife as for military glory. Instead, he walked over to the sideboard to pour her a glass of ratafia in the hopes that it would calm the incessant fluttering of her fan.

"And what is the nature of this ruin?" he prompted.

"The *worst imaginable!*" Anne emphasized in response to his complacent tenor. "Never in my life could I have conceived such misfortune! And to think we must suffer at *her* hands. That—that unspeakable wench. That *wicked harlot.*"

So it was the son and not the daughter, Broadmoor thought to himself. He should have expected it would be Edward, who was four years Juliana's senior but who possessed four fewer years to her maturity.

"You cannot conceive what torment I have endured these past days! And I have had no one, not a soul, to comfort me," Anne lamented, bypassing the ratafia as she worried the floor beneath her feet.

"The engagement to Miss Trindle has been called off?" Broadmoor guessed, slightly relieved for he did not think Edward up to the task of matrimony, even with the dowry of Miss Trindle serving as a handsome incentive. But it displeased him that Edward had not changed his ways.

"Heavens, no! Though it may well happen when the Trindles hear how we have been undone! Oh, but it is the fault of that devil-woman! My poor Edward, to have fallen victim to such a villainous lot."

Broadmoor suppressed a yawn.

"No greater ruin has *ever* befallen a Barrington," Anne added, sensing her nephew did not share her distress.

"Madam, my hostess awaits my attention," he informed her, looking towards the stairs.

Anne burned red as she remembered where she was. "As this was a calamity—yes, a calamity—of the highest order, I could not wait. If your uncle were here, there would have been no need... well, perhaps. His disquiet could often worsen my state. But your presence, Radcliff, affords me hope. I have nowhere else to turn. And you were always quite sensible. I wish that you would learn Edward your ways. You were his trustee and have fifteen more years of wisdom than he. You might take him under your wing."

He raised an eyebrow at the suggestion. "Edward came of age last year when he turned twenty-one. He is master of his own fortune and free to ruin himself as he sees fit."

"How can you speak so?"

"I have intervened once already in Edward's life and have no wish to make a practice of it," Broadmoor replied coolly.

"But…"

He placed the ratafia in her hand before she sank into the nearest sofa, bereft of words in a rare moment for Anne Barrington.

"But that *darkie* is a hundred times worse than her sister!" Anne said upon rallying herself. "Oh, are we never to rid ourselves of this cursed family and their treachery?"

Broadmoor watched in dismay as she set down her glass and began agitating her fan before her as if it alone could save her from a fainting spell. He went to pour himself a glass of brandy, his hopes of a short visit waning.

"What will become of us?" Anne moaned. "What will become of Juliana? I had hopes that she would make a match this year! Did you know that the banns might be read for Miss Helen next month and she has not nearly the countenance that Juliana has!"

"What could Edward have done to place Juliana's matrimonial prospects in jeopardy?" he asked. "Juliana has breeding and beauty and one of the most desirable assets a young woman could have: an inheritance of fifty thousand pounds."

His aunt gave an indignant gasp. Her mouth opened to utter a retort or to comment on her nephew's insensitivity but thought better of it.

"But what are we to do without Brayten?" she asked with such despondency that Broadmoor almost felt sorry for her.

"I beg your pardon?"

"The thought overwhelms me. Indeed, I can scarcely speak, the nature of it is so dreadful…"

He refrained from pointing out the irony in her statement.

"Edward has lost Brayten."

It was Broadmoor's turn to be rendered speechless, but he quickly collected himself and said in a dark voice. "Lost Brayten? Are you sure of this?"

"When I think of the care and attention I lavished upon him— and to be repaid in such a fashion! To be undone in such a manner. And by that wretched harlot. What sort of odious person would prey upon an innocent boy like Edward?"

"Edward is far from innocent," he informed her wryly, "but how is it he could have lost Brayten?"

The boy was reckless, Broadmoor knew, but Brayten was the sole source of income for Edward. The estate had been in the Barrington family for generations and boasted an impressive house in addition to its extensive lands. Surely the boy could not have been so careless as to jeopardize his livelihood.

"It is that witch, that hussy and devil-woman. They say she works magic with the cards. Witchcraft, I say!"

"Do you mean to tell me that Edward lost Brayten in a game of cards?" Broadmoor demanded.

"I had it from Mr. Thornsdale, who came to me at once after it had happened. I would that he had gone to you instead! Apparently, Edward had to wager Brayten to win back his obligation of eighty thousand pounds."

"Eighty thousand pounds!" Broadmoor exclaimed. "He is a bigger fool than I feared."

"I wish you would not speak so harshly of your cousin."

"Madam, I shall have far harsher words when I see him!"

"It is the work of that *harlot*." Anne shook her fan as if to fend off an imaginary foe. "A sorceress, that one. The blood of pagans runs in her veins. Her kind practice the black arts. Yes, that is how she swindled my Edward. She ought to be run out of England!"

He narrowed his eyes. "Of whom do you speak?"

"*Darcy Sherwood*." Anne shuddered. "Her sister and stepmother are the most common of common, but Miss Sherwood is the worst of them all! I hear the Sherwoods are in no small way of debt. No doubt they are only too happy to put their greedy hands upon our precious estate! I wonder that the darkie, that wench, had orchestrated the entire episode to avenge herself for what Edward had done to her sister—as if a gentleman of his stature could possibly look upon such a common young woman with *any* interest."

It had been five years, but Broadmoor remembered the Sherwood name. Only it had been Priscilla Sherwood that had posed the problem then. He had not thought the young lady a suitable match for Edward, who had formed an unexpected attachment to her, and severed the relationship between the two lovebirds by removing his cousin to Paris, where Edward had promptly forgotten about Priscilla in favor of the pretty French girls with their charming accents.

But Broadmoor had only vague recollections of Miss Darcy Sherwood, the elder of the Sherwood sisters.

"Oh, wretched, wretched is our lot!" Anne continued. "To think that we could be turned out of our own home by that piece of jade."

"That will not happen," Broadmoor pronounced, setting down his glass. Perhaps Anne was right and he should have taken more of an interest in Edward's affairs.

Relief washed over Anne. "How grand you are, Radcliff! If anyone can save our family, it is you! Your father and mother, bless their souls, would have been proud of you."

His thoughts turned to the woman upstairs. Penelope would not be pleased, but he meant to have his horse saddled immediately. His first visit would be to Mr. Thornsdale, a trusted friend of the family, to confirm the facts of what Anne had relayed to him.

And if Anne had the truth, his second visit would be to Miss Darcy Sherwood.

That wicked harlot.

CHAPTER TWO

NO ONE NOTICED THE GENTLEMAN sitting in the dark corner of Mrs. Tillinghast's modest card-room. If they had, they would have immediately discerned him to be a man of distinction, possibly a member of the *ton*. His attire was simple but elegant, his cravat sharply tied, his black leather boots polished to perfection. On his right hand, he wore a signet bearing the seal of his title, the Baron Broadmoor.

Upon closer inspection, they would have found the edition of *The Times* that he held before him and pretended to read was over two days old. Why he should be reading the paper instead of participating in the revelry at the card tables was a mystery unto itself. No one came to Mrs. Tillinghast's gaming house to *read*. They came for three distinct reasons: the friendly tables, the surprisingly good burgundy, and a young woman named Miss Darcy Sherwood.

That wicked harlot.

Somewhere in the room a clock chimed the midnight hour, but the wine had been flowing freely for hours, making her partakers deaf to anything but the merriment immediately surrounding them. From the free manner in which the men and women interacted—one woman seemed to have her arse permanently affixed to the lap of her beaux while another boasted a décolletage so low her nipples peered above its lace trim—the Baron wondered that the gaming house might not be better deemed a brothel.

The only person to eventually take notice of Radcliff Barrington was a flaxen-haired beauty, but after providing a curt answer to her greeting without even setting down his paper, he was rewarded with an indignant snort and a return to his solitude. He rubbed his temple as he recalled how he had left the hysterics of his aunt only to be met upstairs with a tirade from his mistress about the impolitesse and hauteur of Anne Barrington to come calling at the residence of a woman she had hitherto acknowledged with the barest of civilities. After noting that the waistcoat upon the chair had disappeared upon his return, Broadmoor had turned the full weight of his stare upon Penelope, who instantly cowered and, upon hearing that he was to take his leave, professed that naturally he must attend to the affairs of his family with due speed.

A lyrical laughter transcending the steady murmur of conversation and merrymaking broke into his reverie. It was followed by a cacophony of men exclaiming "Miss Sherwood! Miss Sherwood!" and begging of said personage to grace their gaming table of faro or piquet. Peering over his paper, Broadmoor paused. For a moment, he could not reconcile the woman he beheld to the devil incarnate his aunt had described.

Miss Darcy Sherwood had a distinct loveliness born of her mixed heritage. The gown of fashion, with its empire waist and diaphanous skirt, accentuated her curves. The pale yellow dress, which Broadmoor noted was wearing thin with wear, would have looked unexceptional on most Englishwomen, but against her caramel toned skin, it radiated like sunshine.

Her hair lacked shine or vibrancy in color, but the abundance of tight full curls framed her countenance with both softness and an alluring unruliness. However, it was her bright brown eyes, fringed with long curved lashes, and her luminous smile that struck Broadmoor the most. It was unlike the demure turn at the corners of the lips that he was accustomed to seeing.

He felt an odd desire to whisk her away from the cads and hounds that descended upon her like vultures about a kill. But this protective instinct was shortlived when he saw her choice of companions was one James Newcastle.

Miss Sherwood could not have been much more than twenty-five years of age. Newcastle was nearly twice that, and it was all but common knowledge that he buggered his female servants, most of whom were former slaves before the British court finally banned the practice from the Isles. But then, the man was worth a hefty sum, having benefitted tremendously from his business in the American slave trade.

"A song, Miss Sherwood!" cried Mr. Rutgers. "I offer twenty quid for the chance to win a song."

"Offer fifty and I shall make it a *private performance*," responded Miss Sherwood gaily as she settled at the card table.

She was no better than a common trollop, Broadmoor decided, trading her favors for money. He felt his blood race to think that the fate of his family rested in the hands of such a hussy. He could tell from the swiftness with which she shuffled, cut, and then dealt the cards that she spent many hours at the tables. Her hands plied the cards like those of an expert pianist over the ivories. He was surprised that her hands could retain such deftness after watching her consume two glasses of wine within the hour and welcome a third. He shook his head.

Shameless.

Broadmoor felt as if he had seen enough of her unrefined behavior, but something about her compelled him to stay. Miss Sherwood, who had begun slurring her words and laughing at unwarranted moments as the night wore on, seemed to enjoy the attentions, but despite her obvious inebriation, her laughter sounded forced. There were instances when he thought he saw sadness in her eyes, but they were fleeting, like illusions taunting the fevered brain.

It was foolhardy for a woman to let down her guard in such company. She would require more than the assistance of the aging butler and scrawny page he had noticed earlier to keep these hounds at bay. Could it possibly be a sense of chivalry that obliged him to stay even as he believed that a woman of her sort deserved the fate that she was recklessly enticing? His family and friends would have been astounded to think it possible.

"My word, but Lady Luck has favored you tonight!" Rutgers exclaimed to Miss Sherwood, who had won her fourth hand in a row.

"Miss Sherwood has been in Her Company the whole week," remarked Mr. Wempole, a local banker, "since winning the deed to Brayten. I daresay you may soon pay off your debts to me."

Broadmoor ground his teeth at the mention of his late uncle's estate and barely noticed the flush that had crept up Miss Sherwood's face.

"It was quite unexpected," Miss Sherwood responded. "I rather think that I might—"

"That were no luck but pure skill!" declared Viscount Wyndham, the future Earl of Brent.

"Alas, I have lost my final pound tonight and have no hope of winning a song from Miss Sherwood," lamented Rutgers.

"I would play one final round," said Miss Sherwood as she shuffled the deck, the cards falling from her slender fingers with a contented sigh, "but brag is best played with at least a fourth."

"Permit me," said Broadmoor, emerging from the shadows. He reasoned to himself that he very much desired to put the chit in her place, but that could only partly explain why he was drawn to her table.

She raised an eyebrow before appraising him with a gaze that swept from the top of his head to the bottom of his gleaming boots. "We welcome all manner of strangers—especially those with ample purses."

Brazen jade, Broadmoor thought to himself as he took a seat opposite her and pulled out his money.

"S'blood," the schoolboy groused immediately after the cards were dealt and reached for a bottle of burgundy to refill his glass.

Glancing up from the three cards he held, Broadmoor found Miss Sherwood staring at him with an intensity that pinned him to his chair. The corners of her mouth turned upward as her head tilted ever so slightly to the side. Looking at her sensuously full lips, Broadmoor could easily see how she had all the men here in the palm of her hand. He wondered, briefly, how those lips would feel under his.

"Our cards are known to be friendly to newcomers," she informed him. "I hope they do not fail to disappoint."

He gave only a small smile. She thought him a naïve novice if she expected him to reveal anything of the hand that he held.

Darcy turned her watchful eye to Newcastle, whose brow was furrowed in deep concentration. She leaned towards him—her breasts nearly grazing the top of the table—and playfully tapped him on the forearm. "Lady Luck can pass you by no longer for surely your patience will warrant her good graces."

Radcliff tried not to notice the two lush orbs pushed and separated above her bodice. He shifted uncomfortably in his seat for despite his inclination to find himself at odds with anything Anne said, he was beginning to believe his aunt. Miss Sherwood possessed a beauty and aura that was like the call of Sirens, luring men to their doom. His own cock stirred with a mind of its own.

His slight movement seemed to catch her eye instantly, but she responded only by reaching for her glass of wine. After taking a long drink, she slammed the glass down upon the table. "Shall we make our last round for the evening the most dramatic, my dears? I shall offer a song—and a kiss…"

A murmur of excitement mixed with hooting and hollering waved over the room.

"…worth a hundred quid," she finished.

"S'blood," the schoolboy grumbled again after opening his purse to find he did not have the requisite amount. He threw his cards onto the table with disgust and grabbed the burgundy for consolation.

Newcastle pulled at his cravat, looked at his cards several times, before finally shaking his head sadly. Miss Sherwood fixed her gaze upon Radcliff next. He returned her stare and fancied that she actually seemed unsettled for the briefest of moments.

Almond brown. Her eyes were almond brown. And despite their piercing gaze, they seemed to be filled with warmth—like the comforting flame of a hearth in winter. Broadmoor decided it must be the wine that leant such an effect to her eyes. How like the Ironies in Life that she should possess such loveliness to cover a black soul.

"Shall we put an end to the game?" Miss Sherwood asked.

"As you please," Broadmoor replied without emotion. Her Siren's call would not work on him. "I will see your cards."

He pulled out two additional hundreds, placing the money on the table with a solemn deliberation that belied his eagerness.

Smiling triumphantly, Miss Sherwood displayed an ace of hearts, a king of diamonds, and a queen of diamonds.

"Though I would have welcomed a win, the joy was in the game," Newcastle said. "I could not derive more pleasure than in losing to you, Miss Sherwood."

Miss Sherwood smiled. "Nor could I ask for a more gallant opponent."

She reached for the money in the middle of the table, but Broadmoor caught her hand.

"It is as you say, Miss Sherwood," he said and revealed a running flush of spades. "Your cards are indeed friendly to newcomers."

For the first time that evening, Broadmoor saw her frown, but she recovered quickly. "Then I presume you will hence no longer be a stranger to our tables?"

Broadmoor was quiet as he collected the money.

"Beginner's luck," the schoolboy muttered.

Newcastle turned his attention to Broadmoor for the first time. "Good sir, I congratulate you on a most remarkable win. I am James Newcastle of Newcastle and Holmes Trading. Our offices are in Liverpool, but you may have heard of the company nonetheless. I should very much like to increase your winnings for the evening by offering you fifty pounds in exchange for Miss Sherwood's song and, er, kiss."

"I believe the song went for fifty and the kiss a hundred," Broadmoor responded.

"Er—yes. A hundred. That would make it a, er, hundred and fifty."

"I am quite content with what I have won. Indeed, I should like to delay no longer my claim to the first of my winnings."

"Very well," said Miss Sherwood cheerfully as she rose. "I but hope you will not regret that you declined the generous offer by Mr. Newcastle."

She headed towards the pianoforte in the corner of the room, but Broadmoor stopped her with his words.

"In *private*, Miss Sherwood."

In contrast to her confident manners all evening, Miss Sherwood seemed to hesitate before flashing him one of her most brilliant smiles. "Of course. But would you not care for a supper first? Or a glass of port in our dining room?"

"No."

"Very well. Then I shall escort you to our humble drawing room."

Broadmoor rose from his chair to follow her. From the corner of his eye, he saw Newcastle looking after them with both longing and consternation. As he passed out of the gaming room, he heard Rutgers mutter, "Lucky bloody bastard."

For a moment Broadmoor felt pleased with having won the game and the image of his mouth claiming hers flashed in his mind. What would her body feel like pressed to his? Those hips and breasts of hers were made to be grabbed...

But hers was a well traversed territory, he reminded himself. Based on his inquiries into Miss Sherwood, the woman changed lovers as frequently as if they were French fashion, and her skills at the card table were matched only by her skills in the bedchamber. The men spoke in almost wistful, tortured tones regarding the latter and often with an odd flush in the cheeks that Broadmoor found strange—and curious.

As with the card-room, the drawing room was modestly furnished. Various pieces were covered with black lacquer to disguise the ordinary quality of their components. A couple giggling in the corner took their leave upon the entry of Miss Sherwood, who closed the door behind him. Sitting down on a sofa that looked as if it might have been an expensive piece at one time but that age had rendered ragged in appearance, he crossed one long leg over another and watched as she went to sit down at the spinet.

Good God, even the way she walked made him warm in the loins. The movement accentuated the flare of her hips and the curve of her rump, neither of which her gown could hide. And yet she possessed a grace on par with the most seasoned ladies at Almack's. She did not walk as much as *glide* towards the spinet.

"Do you care for Mozart?" she asked.

"As you wish," he replied.

She chose an aria from *Le Nozze di Figaro*. The opera buffa with its subject of infidelity and its satirical underpinnings regarding the aristocracy seemed a fitting choice for her. Save for her middling pronunciation of Italian, Miss Sherwood might have done well as an opera singer. She sang with force, unrestrained. The room seemed too small to hold the voice wafting above the chords of the spinet. And she sang with surprising clarity, her fingers striking the keys with precision, undisturbed by the wine he had seen her consume. Despite her earlier displays of inebriation, she now held herself well, and he could not help but wonder if the intoxication had not all been an act.

"My compliments," he said when she had finished. "Though one could have had the entire opera performed for much less than fifty pounds, I can understand why one would easily wager such an amount for this privilege."

"Thank you, but you did so without ever having heard me sing," she pointed out.

She wanted to know why, but he said simply, "I knew I would win."

Her brows rose at the challenge in his tone. The work of the devil could not always prevail. He ought bestir himself now to broach the matter that had compelled him here, but he found himself wanting to collect on the second part of his winnings: the kiss.

She rose from her bench, and his pulse pounded a faster beat. She smiled with the satisfaction of a cat that had sprung its trap on a mouse. "Would you care to test your confidence at our tables some more?"

"Are the bets here always this intriguing?" he returned.

"If you wish," she purred as she stood behind a small decorative table, a safe distance from him.

She began rearranging the flowers in a vase atop the table. "How is it you have not been here before?"

The teasing jade. If she did not kiss him soon, he would have to extract it for himself.

"I did not know its existence until today."

She studied him from above the flowers with a candor and length that no proper young woman would dare, but he did not mind her attempts to appraise him.

"You are new to London?"

Feeling restless, he stood up. He did not understand her hesitation. In the card room she had flaunted herself unabashed to any number of men, but now she chose to play coy with him?

"My preference is for Brooks's," he stated simply. "Tell me, Miss Sherwood, do your kisses always command a hundred pounds?"

Her lower lip dropped. His loins throbbed, and he found he could not tear his gaze from the maddening allure of her mouth.

"Do the stakes frighten you?" she returned.

"I find it difficult to fathom any kiss to be worth that price."

"Then why did you ante?"

"As I've said, I knew I would win."

He could tell she was disconcerted, and when he took a step towards her, she glanced around herself as if in search of an escape.

Finding little room to maneuver, she lifted her chin and smiled. "Then care to double the wager?"

"Frankly, Miss Sherwood, for a hundred pounds, you ought to be offering far more than a kiss."

As I am sure you have done, he added silently. He was standing at the table and could easily have reached across it for her.

Her eyes narrowed at him. No doubt she was more accustomed to men who became simpering puppies at her feet. Perhaps she was affronted by his tone. But he little cared. She was too close to him, her aura more inviting than the scent of the flowers that

separated them. He was about to avail himself of his prize when a
knock sounded at the door.

"Yes?" Miss Sherwood called with too much relief.

The page popped his head into the room. "Mistress Tillinghast
requested a word with you, Miss Sherwood."

Miss Sherwood excused herself and walked past him. The room
became dreary without her presence. Though at first he felt
greatly agitated by the intrusion of the page, he now felt relieved.
He had a purpose in coming here. And instead he was falling
under her spell. Shaking off the warmth that she had engendered
in his body, he forced his mind to the task at hand. Now that he
had gathered his wits about him, he shook his head at himself.
Was it because he had not completed bedding his mistress that he
found himself so easily captivated by Miss Sherwood?

He could see how this place could retain so many patrons and
ensnare those of lesser fortitude and prudence like Edward. Even
Mr. Thornsdale, whom Broadmoor would have thought more at
home at White's than a common gaming hall such as this, revealed
that he had known of Edward's increasing losses to Miss Sherwood
because he himself was an occasional patron. Mr. Thornsdale had
also offered, unsolicited, that he thought Miss Sherwood to be
rather charming.

But Broadmoor doubted that he would find her as charming.
The fourth Baron Broadmoor had a single objective in seeking
out Miss Darcy Sherwood: to wrest from the wicked harlot what
rightfully belonged to his family. And he meant to do so at any
cost.

CHAPTER THREE

❦

"**N**OW WHO DO YOU SUPPOSE that tasty morsel of a stranger be?" wondered Mathilda Tillinghast—dubbed 'Mrs. T' by her gaming hall patrons—as she observed Darcy staring into the vanity mirror. Once a beauty who could summon a dozen men to her feet with a simple drop of her nosegay, Mathilda was now content to use Darcy as the main attraction of the gaming hall. "I find the air of mystery about him quite alluring."

"I thought for certain that I had correctly appraised his position," Darcy said, still wondering how she had lost that hand of brag. She had begun working at the gaming hall ever since her father, Jonathan Sherwood, had passed away ten years ago and left the family the remains of a sizeable debt, and rarely misjudged an opponent. What was it about the stranger that had sent her thoughts scattering like those of a schoolgirl?

She was both intrigued and unsettled by him. Instead of luring him into more rounds at the card tables—and the kiss would have been a perfect bait with any other man—she found herself *timid*. Mathilda would have found it incomprehensible that she, Darcy Sherwood, who had taken many a man to her bed in more ways than most women could imagine, should be afraid of a simple kiss. When the page had appeared, she could not wait to escape and was now reluctant to leave the refuge of Mathilda's boudoir.

"How could I have lost?" she wondered aloud.

Mathilda snorted. "You sound as if you were in mourning, m'dear. Tisn't as if you lost any money. Wouldn't mind taking your place, in fact. Would that I were your age again. Give you a run for your money I would, 'cept for Newcastle maybe—you can have him."

Darcy shuddered. "If he had not boasted of how well his former slaves were treated—'better than courtesans,' were his words—and then to say that these women ought to be grateful for his kindness—I might have developed a conscience towards him. But knowing that his wealth comes from that horrible trade that ought to be outlawed if only Parliament would listen to Sir Wilberforce, I have no remorse of relieving him of some of that money."

"He can easily afford it, m'dear. They all deserve what they get if they are fool enough to fall for a pretty face."

"Who deserves it?" blurted Henry Perceville, Viscount Wyndham, as he entered the room unannounced and threw himself on the rickety bed. Despite his slender build, the mattress promptly sank beneath his weight. His golden locks fell across a pair of eyes that sparkled with merriment.

"Men," Mathilda answered.

"Nonetheless," said Darcy as she tucked an unruly curl behind her ear, "I should be relieved to give up the charade and restore what little dignity is left for me. Never to have to counterfeit another interested smile or to feign enjoyment at being fondled by every Dick and Harry…to be free…"

"You have the means to end the charade this instant—you have the deed to Brayten!" protested Henry.

"Which I mean to return. I feel as if I have fleeced a babe."

Henry rolled his eyes. "What a ninny you are. Edward Barrington is no innocent, as evidenced by what he did to your sister."

Darcy pressed her lips into a firm line. It had been five years, but the wound flared as strong as ever. She adored her sister Priscilla, her junior by four years, and whom she had always sought to protect. Edward had not only wronged Priscilla, but in so doing, had wronged Nathan, an innocent boy born without a father.

"How you can have the slightest sympathy for that pup confounds me," agreed Mathilda.

"I will never forgive the Barringtons for their mistreatment of Priscilla," Darcy acknowledged. "But I could not send a man and his family to ruin in such a fashion."

"That folly were his own creation. It was not your idea to offer up his own estate for a wager."

"If I offer to return Brayten in exchange for what Edward had initially lost to me, I could pay off our debts to Mr. Wempole and have enough to live comfortably for many years. Eighty thousand pounds were no paltry sum."

Henry threw his legs off the bed and sat up to face Darcy. "I am your oldest and dearest friend, and I must say that if you dare return Brayten to that Barrington fellow, I will never speak to you again. At the very least, wait a sennight before making your mind."

"Make the rascal squirm a might," agreed Mathilda. "I had meant to tell you that Mr. Reynolds has returned, and I think he is willing to open his purse a great deal more tonight—with the appropriate persuasion, of course. But this delectable stranger is far more promising."

Darcy blushed, turning away but not before Henry noticed.

"Do my eyes deceive?" he inquired. "Are you interested in this fellow?"

"He is different," Darcy admitted, recalling the most intense pair of eyes she had ever seen.

"Simply because a man refrains from ogling you or pawing you does not make him different from the others, darling. Oldest trick in the book."

"Am I not old enough to know all manner of tricks?" Darcy replied. "It amuses me how often men overestimate the appeal of their sex."

"They serve their purpose," added Mathilda with an almost sentimental wistfulness before taking a practical tone, "but like a banquet, one must sample a variety. Our Darcy will not be turned by one man alone, no matter how appetizing he appears."

"The only use I have of men, save you, dear Harry, is their pocketbooks," said Darcy firmly before taking her leave.

Despite her parting words, however, before returning to the drawing room where *he* waited, Darcy stopped at a mirror in the hallway to consider her appearance. She found herself concerned with how the stranger might perceive her. An entirely silly feeling more appropriate to a chit out of the schoolroom than an experienced woman such as herself. She wasn't even sure that the man liked her. Indeed, she rather suspicioned that he did not, despite his having wagered for her kiss. Nonetheless, she confirmed that the sleeves of her gown were even and that her hair was tucked more or less in place.

"Never thought to find you here, Lord Broadmoor."

It was the voice of Cavin Richards, a notorious rake known among women for his seductive grin and among men for his many female conquests.

Broadmoor, Darcy repeated to herself. The name was vaguely familiar.

"And your presence here surprises me none at all," was the uninterested response from the stranger in the drawing room.

Not put off, Cavin replied, "Yes, I find White's and Brooks's rather dull in comparison to Mrs. T.'s. Care for a round of hazard?"

"I came not for cards or dice but to see Miss Sherwood."

"Ahhhh, of course, *Miss Sherwood.*"

Darcy was familiar with the suggestive smile that Cavin was no doubt casting at the stranger. She held herself against the wall but inched closer towards the open doors.

"Quite pleasurable to the eye, is she not?" Cavin drawled.

"She is tolerable."

"Tolerable? My friend, you are either blind in an eye or have odd standards of beauty."

"While I find her appearance does no offense, it cannot hide the vulgarity of her nature."

Darcy bit her bottom lip. She supposed she had played the flirt quite heavily tonight, but had she been that offensive?

"Vulgarity of nature?" Cavin echoed. "I agree Miss Sherwood is no candidate for Almack's but that's playing it up strong. Or is it her vulgarity what draws you? I must say, I never saw that side of you, Broadmoor. I own that I thought you rather a bore, but now you intrigue me!"

The irritation in his voice was evident as Broadmoor responded, "It is clear to me that you know little of me, Richards, and perhaps less of Miss Sherwood or even you would not be so ready to consort in her company. I know your standards to be *pliant,* but I did not think they would extend to the lowest forms of humankind. Indeed, I would barely put Miss Sherwood above the snail or any other creature that crawls with its belly to the earth. For beauty or not, I would rather be seen with a carnival animal than in her company. It is with the greatest displeasure that circumstances have compelled—nay, forced—me to call upon her. I would that I had nothing to do with her, her family, or any of her ilk."

"Then what extraordinary occasion would bring my lordship from his Olympus to consort with us lower mortals?" Darcy asked upon her appearance in the drawing room, relieved that her voice did not quiver quite as much as she had feared it would for it was difficult to contain the anger that flared within her.

The Baron seemed taken aback but quickly collected himself. His bow to her was exceedingly low, but the ice in his tone would have sent shivers down the most stalwart man. "Miss Sherwood, I have matters to dispense that I trust will not require much of your time or mine."

He turned to Cavin and added, "In private."

Darcy could tell from his eager expression that her former lover desired very much to stay, but she had no interest in his presence either.

"My invitation to hazard remains open should you decide to stay," Cavin told Broadmoor as he picked up his hat and gloves, winking at Darcy before departing.

With Cavin gone, Darcy placed the full weight of her gaze upon the Baron. She lifted her chin as if that alone gave her height enough to match his.

"I think you know why I have come to call," Broadmoor said without a wasted second.

"It was not for my song?" She hoped her flippant tone covered how much his earlier words had stung her.

"Do not play your games with me, my child."

Games? What was he getting at?

"Then what game do you wish to play, sir, brag apparently not being sufficient for you?"

Her response seemed to ignite flames in his eyes. He took a menacing step towards her, his lips pressed into a thin line. "It would be unwise of you to incur my wrath."

"And you mine," she responded before thinking. She was not about to allow him browbeat her.

He looked surprised, then amused to the point of laughter. She took that moment to move towards the sideboard for despite her desire to challenge him word for word and gaze for gaze, his nearness was beginning to intimidate her.

"I am prepared to offer a great sum for the return of the deed to Brayten," he announced. "I am told that the circumstances of the wager between you and my cousin were fair. For that reason alone, I offer recompense."

It was then that Darcy recognized the eyes—the same color of coal as Edward Barrington, who sported much lighter hair and whose lanky form did not match his cousin's imposing physique. Her mind sank into the recesses of her mind to connect the name of Broadmoor with one Radcliff Barrington.

She had heard only that his manner tended towards the aloof. She should not be surprised that, like his cousin, he tended towards the arrogant as well, but nothing had quite prepared her for the condescension that overflowed with each deliberate word of his.

"Pray, what great sum are you offering?" she asked with nonchalance as she poured herself a glass of burgundy.

"The proposal of a monetary recompense interests you, I see," he noted.

How she wished she could turn the lout into stone with her glare. Instead, she feigned a sweet smile and said, "Yes, we lower creatures of the earth prefer the petty and base interests."

"I am prepared to offer one hundred thousand pounds, Miss

Sherwood."

Darcy began choking on the wine she had tried to imbibe just then. After coughing and sputtering and feeling as if her face must have matched her beverage in color, she straightened herself.

One hundred thousand pounds…it was enough to discharge the debts and provide a decent living for her family. By returning Brayten, her intention from the start, she could have done with the gaming house. She was tempted to take his offer without a second thought, but various words he had said rang in her head. Had he called her a child earlier?

"Your cousin was in debt to me for eighty thousand pounds before he lost Brayten," she said, stalling. "One could say you are offering me only twenty thousand pounds for Brayten. I think the estate to be worth far more than that, surely?"

His eyes were flint, and her heart beat faster as she tried to ignore the way his stare bored into her.

"What sum would you find more appropriate?"

The question stumped Darcy. She had no impression of what Brayten could actually be worth.

"Two hundred thousand pounds?" she guessed.

This time it was Broadmoor's turn to choke and turn color. "You are refreshingly forthright of your greed. I have known many indulgent people in the course of my life, but you, Miss Sherwood, are the epitome of cupidity!"

"And you, sir, are the epitome of insolence!" she returned.

As if sensing that the gloves had come off, Broadmoor sneered, "I am relieved to discard our pretenses of civility. My courtesy is wasted on a wanton jade."

"If you think your impertinence will aid your efforts to reclaim Brayten at a lower sum, you are a poor negotiator!"

"My offer stems from my generosity. I could easily consult my barristers and find another means of retrieving what is mine."

"Then speak to your barristers and do not misuse my time!"

The words flew from her mouth before she had a chance to consider them. She wondered for a moment if she were being unwise but then decided she didn't care.

In his displeasure, he clenched his jaw, causing a muscle in his face to ripple. "You may find my cousin easy prey, but I assure you that I am no fool."

"How comforting," Darcy could not resist.

"Impudent trollop! I have a mind to drag you into the street for a public whipping!"

Unable to fend off her anger, Darcy glared at him and declared, "You have persuaded me that to part with Brayten for anything less than three hundred thousand pounds would be folly."

"Jezebel! Are there no limits to your wickedness?"

Darcy shrugged and looked away. Her heart was pounding madly.

"I see plainly what is afoot," Broadmoor observed. "You mean to punish me for taking Edward from your sister."

She glanced sharply at him. "You! You took Edward?"

"A most wise decision on my part, for I would rather see him in hell than attached to a family such as yours!"

Her heart grew heavy as she remembered Priscilla's pain and thought of the life that should have been afforded to Nathan had Edward done right by them both.

And it was apparently the doing of Edward's arrogant cousin!

"I would not return Brayten to you for the world!" Darcy cried. "If I were a man, I should throw you from the house. You are a lout and a mucker!"

He took a furious step towards her. "You ought consider yourself fortunate, Miss Sherwood, not to be a man else I would not hesitate to box your ears in. You do not deserve the decency afforded to a trull..."

A trull was she? A Jezebel. A jade. She had heard worse, but coming from him, the words were fuel to a fire already burning out of control. What else was it that he had said? *For beauty or not, I would rather be seen with a carnival animal than in her company...*

"I will consider your exchange under one condition," she said. "You will submit to being my suitor—*an ardent suitor*—for a period of six months. You will tend to my every wish and command. Only then, upon your satisfactory and unconditional submission, will I relinquish the deed to Brayten."

He stared at her in disbelief before smirking. "You suffer delusions of grandeur. I am not in the habit of courting sluts."

"Then I suggest you begin practicing," she replied, feeling triumphant to see the veins in his neck pulsing rapidly. "You will appear no later than ten o'clock each evening and await my directions. You will speak not a word of this arrangement to anyone or I am sure to find Brayten beautiful this time of year."

Broadmoor was beyond livid. He grabbed her with both of his hands. "Damnable doxy! I shall see you thrown in gaol for your treachery and have no remorse if you perished there."

He was holding her so close that she could feel his angry breath upon her cheek. She tried to ignore the rapid beating of her heart and the painful manner in which her arms were locked in his vice. He looked as if he desired to snap her in twain—and could no doubt accomplish it rather easily in his current state of wrath. It took all her courage to force out words.

"Unhand me, Baron—lest you wish to pay for the privilege of your touch."

At first he drew her closer. Darcy held her breath. But then he threw her from him in disgust as if she possessed a contagion. Grabbing his gloves and cane, he strode out of the room. Darcy watched his anger with pleasure, but a small voice inside warned her that she had just awoken a sleeping tiger.

CHAPTER FOUR

&

AUNT DARCY…I CAME ACROSS MRS. Weaver, who is not of any lineage that signifies but you would never know it from the airs she gives herself…the largest dog I ever saw…with the most audacious headdress…

"Aunt Darcy!"

Darcy Sherwood snapped to attention and looked across the dining table into the bright eyes of her five year old nephew. Each day Nathan grew more and more like Edward Barrington. The boy had the same dark eyes, the same ears that curved outward from his face, the same rounded jaw. He had his mother's fair hair and her sweet smile, but excepting those features, he was a diminutive version of his father. Darcy had vowed that the similarities would lie only with his physiognomy. He was better off with as little of the Barrington blood in him as possible.

She knew not which Barrington was worse: Edward or his cousin Radcliff. She had not slept well the night before for she could not rid herself of the image of the Baron Broadmoor, gazing down his nose at her with those dark unnerving eyes of his. And when she awoke, her first thoughts had been of his rugged countenance—she would make that handsome scorn of his turn into a frown of despair—and his blistering words—he would be speechless when she was through with him. And to think she had nearly kissed the man! Worse—she had desired it. Her body soured recalling how giddy and anxious she had felt yesterday before he revealed his true purpose. If he had meant all that he had said, why the bloody hell had he bothered playing that hand of brag? Was it to humiliate her? The thought burned her, and she could hardly wait to provide him his set-down.

"Aunt Darcy, did you hear my story?"

"Let Darcy eat in peace," admonished a slender and pretty young woman of two and twenty years.

"Worry not, Priscilla. I enjoy my supper with a story," Darcy assured her sister. She turned to Nathan. "Will you tell it to me again?"

Nathan smiled. "Most certainly!"

"I take it you heard not a word I said either?" asked Mrs. Sherwood with a self-pitying sniff as she dabbed at the corners of her mouth so as not to mar the rouge upon her lips. Leticia Sherwood always kept her face presentable as if important company might call upon them at any moment.

"Mama, you ought not to have bought a new bonnet," replied Priscilla, "no matter what Mrs. Weaver said. You yourself said she gives herself airs. Even were she any authority on the fashion of bonnets, we haven't the money for such expenditures."

"Does this mean we can't have a dog either?" asked Nathan.

"I fear it is."

The crestfallen look on the boy's face pained Darcy. It was not the first time he had been denied, and for the most part he bore the realities like a little soldier. He never complained that his meals were plain, his clothes worn, his playthings nearly nonexistent, but a dog was something he had set his heart on.

"No matter how good I am?" Nathan persisted.

Darcy caught her sister's helpless look and responded, "Someday, Nathan. It may be longer than you wish, but someday, you shall have a dog."

"Then I shall be especially good—shall I?—so that day may come!" exclaimed Nathan happily. "Mama, as I have finished my plate, shall I go wash the dishes?"

Darcy watched her nephew depart with both pride and pain. As little girls, neither she nor Priscilla had ever had to work in the kitchen. Jonathan Sherwood had made a decent sum in the

West Indies, where Darcy was born, and there had been plenty of servants in the Sherwood house. Now Priscilla and Mrs. Sherwood shared a maid between them. The butler, the housekeeper, the footmen, and all the other maids had been dismissed before Nathan was born. Darcy had tried as hard as she could to retain at least the house they had lived in, but the income at the gaming hall and what loans she could secure would not suffice.

Priscilla turned her bright blue eyes, fringed with long full lashes, onto Darcy. "How in the world are we to afford a dog when we can barely feed the three mouths currently under this roof—let alone an animal that could easily eat the equivalent of two?"

"We can afford a dog and new bonnets. Darcy holds the deed to Brayten!" declared Mrs. Sherwood triumphantly. "I have often said that gaming hell you frequent is despicable. I thought for certain that nothing good could ever come of your being there, but Providence has at last seen fit to pity our situation."

Priscilla glanced at Darcy in surprise. "I thought you meant to return the deed?"

Darcy took a bite of her stale bread and chewed it vehemently as the image of the Baron Broadmoor flashed before her eyes. "In due time."

"Return it?" gasped Mrs. Sherwood. "Why should we wish to return such a prize? What folly! Indeed, no price could compensate us for the wrong they've done to our family!"

"Mama, I am content that the past remain in the past."

"We have a right—your son Nathan—has a right to that land!"

"But it is Darcy that has won it." Priscilla turned to her sister with eyes of regret. "You have born the burden of my mistake. It was my fault—"

"No," Darcy stopped her. She stared hard at her half sister. The two could not look more unalike—one was fair with delicate features, the other dark and dramatic—but Darcy had always felt naught but love for Priscilla. She had cherished playing the little mother to her younger sister. "Edward had the opportunity to do right by you and Nathan, and he chose not to because of that dreadful cousin of his."

"His cousin Radcliff? How do you mean?"

"I only just—the man himself admitted as much to me."

"He came to see you? Oh, Darcy, do be careful! I have only heard stern things said of him."

"Did he try to take Brayten from us?" asked Mrs. Sherwood apprehensively.

"He does not frighten me," Darcy answered, "nor shall he reclaim the deed so easily."

"What do you mean?" Priscilla asked.

Avoiding her sister's worried question, Darcy said, "Do not fret, Priscilla. You imagine yourself—and Nathan—a burden when he is a blessing in our lives. In truth, it is the debt of our dear Papa that weighs upon us—though we do not aid ourselves by contin- uously purchasing items that we can ill afford. And you may think the gaming hall a terrible place, but I quite enjoy it, I assure you. As for Radcliff Barrington, he is of no consequence."

She spoke with greater confidence than she felt where the Baron Broadmoor was concerned, but Darcy had no intention of sharing her plans with either Priscilla or her stepmother. She admired her sister's ability to forgive, but she herself desired only to avenge her family upon Radcliff Barrington. He would regret he had ever crossed swords with Darcy Sherwood.

ℭ

"DO YOU SUPPOSE JONATHAN BANKS will allow me the pleasure of his company this evening?" Henry won- dered aloud to Darcy.

Darcy looked across the card room at the young gentleman in question flirting with one of the female patrons. "Are you sure he can be persuaded?"

"He has yet to discover his true nature, but he can be persuaded. Most assuredly." Henry turned to see who had just entered the room. "That one, I have a distinct feeling, can *not* be persuaded."

Glancing up from the checks she had collected from the last round of faro, Darcy saw the tall form of the Baron Broadmoor. Her heart quickened its beat, and she could not help but admire how the tailoring of his clothes enhanced his impressive figure. The cutaway of his dark blue coat revealed a broad chest encased in a buff waistcoat and immaculate linen. The tall standing collar reached into his lush black hair and was wrapped with a cravat that would have met the approval of Beau Brummel.

She had half expected the Baron not to come, that he would laugh off or simply refuse her ultimatum. From the frown on his face, it was clear he was unhappy to be here. *Good*, she thought to herself. He would soon be unhappier still.

"Another round, Miss Sherwood! The night is young!" cried one of the bettors.

"Soon enough," answered Darcy as she met the gaze of the Baron, "but first I mean to take a respite in the dining hall."

A number of men quickly offered to escort her, but Darcy kept her eyes on Broadmoor. He met her challenging look and presented his arm. His intent stare could easily have been mistaken for determination, but Darcy knew better. She accepted his arm with a satisfied smile.

"Gentleman, actions speak louder than words," she explained before allowing Broadmoor to lead her towards the dining hall.

"How many poor fools have you led to ruin at your faro table?" asked Broadmoor.

"Is that your best attempt at polite conversation?" Darcy returned as he pulled out a chair for her at one of the more private dining tables. No doubt he desired to be seen by as few people as possible.

"My impression is that polite conversation is the least of your interests here."

"Ah, yes, we do our share of gambling here as well. I am sure you have noted that this *is* a gaming house?"

"Is that all it is?" he replied with a cocked eyebrow.

Darcy narrowed her eyes at him. He sat opposite her with his arms crossed, casually leaning against the back of his chair. His posture struck her as arrogant. But even with his mouth curled in a derisive smirk, he was disconcertingly attractive. It was unjust that such a horrible ogre could possess such devilishly handsome features.

"What are you implying, Baron?"

"The men...the women..."

"We are not a priggish establishment. Men and women are free to enjoy each other's company, but we are *not* a brothel."

"Indeed?"

He poured a glass of wine for her from the bottle that had been set at their table. Darcy observed how his fingers curled about the neck of the bottle and was reminded of how strong they had felt when he had grabbed her yesterday. She wondered if those hands were capable of a different kind of touch...if they could stroke as well as grasp...but her thoughts were soon shattered by his next question.

"Is what you do so different from that of a harlot?"

She stared at him in almost disbelief. The gall of this man! But she managed to smile as if she were an amused mother who had just heard her young child say something precocious.

"A whore lies with a man for money," she explained before leaning in and continuing in a conspiratorial tone, "I lay men *for the enjoyment of it.*"

Seeing that she had him speechless, she settled back in her chair with satisfaction. "Make no mistake, Baron, as much as I enjoy the carnal pleasures, I lay only men who may please me. Only no man has managed to please me for long. Which is why I am no courtesan. I prefer my freedom to choose as I please. I am not now and will never be any man's mistress."

"As such, you do very well for Madam Tillinghast," responded Broadmoor, "though it also helps when the dealing boxes are gaffed."

Darcy thought she had mastered the situation, but his words had the effect of completely dispelling her complacency. She bit her tongue—in anger as much as to prevent herself from unleashing a string of invectives.

"Our tables are honest, sir," she said between clenched teeth.
"And the dealers?"

Darcy could not resist jumping to her feet. His raised eyebrow suggested that he was playing her, but nonetheless, he had uttered words that could not be taken lightly in a gaming house. Had she been a man, she would have called him out.

"More honest than some of our patrons," Darcy said, almost quivering with anger. "Though in some cases, cheating would be quite unnecessary on our part. Your cousin, for example, could not win a hand were the game rigged in his favor!"

"Did you not wish to partake of any refreshments?" he called to her after she had turned to leave.

Even that simple question served to ignite her indignation. What was it about him that grated her nerves like no other? she wondered as she stormed out of the dining hall.

"My dear!" Henry exclaimed when she collided with him in the hallway. "You look as if you're ready to take someone's head off."

"I am!" Darcy admitted. "Would you believe what that pompous Baron Broadmoor dared accuse me of? He said...oh, it should not matter. Nothing a Barrington says should ever matter to me."

"I take it this Barrington is even worse than his cousin for I have never seen you this livid. It is not a becoming color on you, my dear."

"Harry, he is far worse than Edward! He is easily the most detestable man I have ever met!"

For the rest of the evening, Darcy refused to engage anymore with the Baron. She did not even wish to make eye contact, though she could not refrain from glancing at him when she thought he wasn't looking. As much as she wanted to embarrass him further, her infuriation had melted her plans for the Baron— at least for now.

You may have won this round, Darcy silently told the man, but tomorrow will see my reprisal two-fold.

Thinking of ways to humiliate the man improved her outlook. Still, she took an early leave of the evening and retired to the bedroom that Mathilda had set up for her long ago so that Darcy would not have to travel through the streets of London at night.

Back in her room, Darcy rang for the abigail that she shared with Mathilda and began to unpin her hair, trying not to think of the Baron Broadmoor and how she could possibly have found him attractive. The intensity of his stare when first she saw him had intrigued her, and it had been some time since any man had caught her attention. She fancied he had not been immune to her charms, but alas, how wrong she had been!

After ringing for the abigail for the third time, Darcy realized she was to have no help undressing for the evening. She removed her gown and with some difficulty managed to disengage her corset. She stepped out of her chemise and into her nightgown. Her hair had already been released from its chignon and fell thickly over her shoulders. She climbed into bed and was about to blow out the candle when a voice jolted her upright.

"Tire of all the amusement already?"

Darcy looked into the semidarkness to see the Baron sitting in a corner chair. Had he been here this whole time? His cravat had been loosened and a small part of his chest could be seen above his shirt.

Her eyes narrowed. "Are you in the habit of stealing into the rooms of ladies?"

He snorted. "Is there a lady present?"

"Get out," Darcy seethed, trying not to think about how much of her undressing he might have witnessed.

He stood up and advanced towards the bed. "But how unkind of you to rebuff one who is but attempting to be, as you demand, an ardent suitor."

"I expected a gentleman suitor."

"Perhaps I am not gentleman where you are concerned. Nor do you deserve a gentleman."

"Pray do not fancy that you can seduce me. I shall ring for the servants."

"And will they come?"

Despite her anger, Darcy paled in the flickering candlelight. She had no doubt that the impudent abigail was simply ignoring her.

The Baron had reached the bed. He scowled down at Darcy. "What did you expect bringing me here and into such company?"

Darcy turned from him and pretended to settle into her pillows, "Do as you will, but I will bid you good night."

To her dismay, Broadmoor slid into bed next to her. "You asked me to play my role convincingly."

"You disturb my sleep, Baron." It sounded stupid, but it was all she could think to say.

Undeterred, Broadmoor slipped a hand down her nightgown and reached for her breast. Darcy stopped his hand.

"How dare you take such liberties?" she gasped harshly, but her body had already begun to warm at his touch.

"From what I understand, others have taken far more liberty than this."

"Only by those who can please me," Darcy responded evenly as she shoved his hand back to him.

"And you think I could not?"

Darcy glared at him. He took her silence as a challenge and reached underneath the covers. His hand grazed her ankle. She started but was overcome by both curiosity and desire to see what he would do next. His hand trailed lightly up her calf and underneath the hem of her gown. She should stop him before he went beyond her calf, but when his fingers brushed the back of her knee, she could not find words. His hand continued lightly up the length of her thigh. When his fingers reached the nest of curls between her legs, she lost a breath.

He was looking at her, but the best she could do was to still any expression in her face. Her mind had been enveloped by the throbbing in her lower body. It yearned for him to continue. After a brief delay, his forefinger slipped to that most exquisite nub of flesh, teasing it to life.

Perhaps she had had more wine than she intended. Or perhaps it was because it had been too long. Though she had not been above bringing herself to satisfaction, it differed from the touch of a man. Somehow, the larger fingers, more imprecise, managed to flare greater sensations. And despite herself, they were beginning to flame with each stroke. Without knowing, she released a soft, almost imperceptible moan, as she lost the will to resist the desires of her own body.

Sensing her surrender, Broadmoor dipped his fingers into her wetness and began a rhythmic stroking of her now engorged bud. Darcy sank into the pillows and closed her eyes, allowing his caresses to draw her deeper and deeper into that familiar and ironic pleasure—a yearning that satisfied, a craving made more intense with each attempt to satiate. His fingers plied her with teasing tenderness, then increasing earnest as her climax began to build. This was madness, she knew, but all rational thought had been pushed aside. Despite herself, she cried out softly in her release.

His fingers slowed but did not stop their caress. Darcy kept her eyes closed as she savored the satisfaction of a craving met. The Baron was no novice lover, though she should not be surprised that this was the case. Even the most pious gentleman could entertain lovers, provided they were discreet, and still maintain their status as a gentleman. It differed quite unfairly for women.

"I take it that pleased my lady?" asked Broadmoor.

"A little," Darcy murmured.

"We must be sure then."

His strokes skimmed her arousal. Darcy shuddered. She should put a stop to this. Should she not? Was he not the man she loathed above all others?

But her body was to betray her once more as the desire between her legs flared anew. He had slipped a finger inside her even while he kept his thumb circling against her. For a moment she tensed as her mind struggled to gain dominance. It lasted briefly. When he intensified his touch, she found herself heading to a climax even higher than before. Her entire body shook. She lay with her eyes closed, soaking in the afterglow. And before she could rouse herself from her state of relief and bliss, she fell asleep.

When she awoke half an hour later, she was alone with no trace that Broadmoor had been present save for the lingering wetness between her legs. She imagined the smug satisfaction that must be on his face at having seduced her. Well, if he meant to play the game that way, she had her own cards in store for the proud Baron.

CHAPTER FIVE

⁕

RADCLIFF THREW THE COLD WATER onto his face and took a ragged breath as it dripped from his hair back into the basin. It failed to wash away the memory of her. The feel of her. The scent of her. The sound of her. Those soft lilting moans echoed even now in his ears, causing the blood in his groin to throb. He was surprised at the intensity of his desire given that he had already relieved his arousal twice since arriving home late last night.

He felt a mixture of shame and triumph. Never in his life would he have thought it possible of himself to enter into a woman's bedchamber without her knowledge and then refuse to leave. But there was no denying that there was something about Miss Sherwood that ignited a brazenness he never knew existed. Something that had nothing to do with her reputation as a harlot of sorts, but everything to do with the way she looked at him.

He had not intended to catch her undressing last night. Surprised that his customarily high sense of decency had not compelled him to excuse himself the moment she began untying her ribbons, he had sat in the dark corner of her room unable to take his eyes off her. He had watched the dress as it fell down her shoulders and past her rounded hips, glimpsed her bare stomach and naked breasts, and was then briefly treated to the curvature of her derriere before her nightdress descended from overhead.

His only thought at first had been to make her as uncomfortable as she had made him. If she desired him to act her suitor, so be it. He would play the part to her great unease. That he should force his company upon her was of her own doing. And, he thought with satisfaction, it was clear she did not completely revile his presence.

She had not seemed overly furious—perturbed, yes, but not frightened by his presence. He had half expected her to scream or attempt to ring for the servants. But when she displayed such nonchalance, he found he could not resist. He had to touch her. Had to please her. Had to teach her a lesson.

It surprised him how intoxicating her reactions were. He would have easily spent the entire night bringing her to spend time and time again had she not fallen asleep. He had been grateful that she had for he was beginning to doubt his own ability to curb the lust that had welled up in his body. His hand ached to touch her again.

Radcliff threw another handful of water at himself before reaching for the linen. After a shave and change of clothing, he went down for his breakfast.

"Any word from Wempole?" he asked his secretary as he consumed the ham, toast, eggs, and beans as if he had not eaten in days.

"No, my lord," responded the gentleman, "but I am told he will back in London in a few days."

After breakfast Radcliff decided to pay another visit to his cousin, who had taken leave of London shortly after his embarrassing loss to Miss Sherwood but was reportedly back in town.

"Wake him," Radcliff instructed the butler, who had opened the door and explained that his master was still asleep.

Radcliff waited five minutes, then took himself into Edward's bedchamber.

"Fiend seize it…" grumbled the young man in bed as he peered at Radcliff through half closed eyes, his soft brown hair tousseled about his boyish face. He was still in his dressing gown and beneath the bed covers. "It's not even noon yet."

Radcliff tossed open the curtains, flooding the room with light.

"I came to inform you," he began as he sat in a chair opposite his cousin's bed, "that I am placing your accounts—including

Brayten—in a trust till you are deemed responsible enough to assume their command."

Edward sat up. "I say! That is most unnecessary, Radcliff!"

"You shall have an allowance of three thousand a year."

"Three?! That is hardly enough to sustain a man."

"Provided you refrain from stepping foot into Mrs. T's or any other gaming hell."

"I shan't agree to this."

"You will if you expect me to secure the return of Brayten."

"And since when do you serve as my guardian?" sniffed Edward indignantly.

"Since you lost your estate to Miss Sherwood," answered Radcliff, though he felt himself in part to blame for not having taken a more active role in Edward's development since the last time he had intervened in the matter of Priscilla Sherwood.

As if reading his cousin's mind, Edward ventured with some hesitation to say, "I had thought perhaps to speak with the sister of Miss Sherwood…"

Broadmoor raised an eyebrow.

"…as she did hold a tendre for me once."

"I thought you had said she was madly in love with you."

"Yes, well…"

"And that she meant to 'even the score' against you," Radcliff continued "It is clear to me the sentiments Miss Sherwood holds towards you. I can only imagine it worse with Miss Priscilla."

"Oh, but Priscilla is quite different from Darcy."

Radcliff crossed his arms. "Indeed?"

Edward looked away quickly. "I meant, well, they are both, er, indiscriminate as regards their lovers. Prime articles they are. I am quite grateful that you, er, helped me to realize that my youthful fancy to Miss Priscilla was greatly misplaced—but I think Miss Sherwood…well, she is in part descended from savages."

"Have you any idea who the father of the boy is?"

Edward colored and shook his head. "Haven't the foggiest."

Radcliff stood and surveyed his cousin with mixed emotions. "I suggest you leave any correspondence with the Sherwoods to me."

"If you think it best, Radcliff. Will you be attending Lady Pinkerton's dinner tonight?"

"I have…another engagement," replied Radcliff and took his leave before Edward decided to ask what that engagement was.

Naturally, it involved Miss Darcy Sherwood.

When Radcliff arrived at Mrs. T's later that evening, he found her laughing at something James Newcastle had whispered in her ear. Radcliff felt the hairs on the back of his neck stand on end. Why should it bother him that she flirted with the buffoon? Still, he could not repress a sudden desire to grab Newcastle by the collar and toss the man out on his head.

There was not a seat to be had near Miss Sherwood, so Radcliff entertained himself at one of the other faro tables from which he could keep on eye on her. It was not easy for one of the women at his table, decidedly tipsy, kept leaning in towards him, soliciting his advice on which card to play. She was not as drunk nor as stupid as she pretended to be, and he had little tolerance of women who felt the need to be inane in the presence of men.

He felt her hand upon his thigh beneath the table and was about to say something offending when he saw that the men around Miss Sherwood had risen to their feet. Leaving his ante on his table, Radcliff strode over to Miss Sherwood who had declared her intention to head to the dining room.

"Are you in need of an escort?" he asked.

She stared at him with a peculiar glint in her eyes. "If I grant you that privilege twice in two nights, people will think I play favorites. I *never* have favorites, Baron."

She turned and took the arm of James Newcastle, who grinned idiotically from ear to ear.

"May I join your table then?" Radcliff persisted, satisfied that Newcastle's smile turned quickly into a frown.

"Perhaps another time."

It was not the last of her rejections that evening. He played the part of the attentive suitor, but she rebuffed his offer to get her a glass of wine as well as his request for a round of piquet.

She kept him at bay all evening, and all he could do for the most part was watch her from afar. It was becoming difficult to bear, in part because she was succeeding in her efforts to humiliate him—something the Baron was not accustomed to feeling—but also because images of the prior evening kept returning to him. He realized he was lusting after her like some predator that could smell but not taste its meat. It made him feel more animal than man.

He decided he had done his best that evening at being one of her supplicants and turned his focus away from Miss Sherwood. He had a glass of wine and played a few rounds of hazard. Occasionally he glanced her way, and once or twice their gazes met across the dim and smoky room. She had something in store for him, he felt. But the hours dragged on, and Radcliff was falling asleep in the armchair that he had favored at his first visit to Mrs. T's when the page handed him a note from Miss Sherwood.

It was a simple command for him to come to her chambers.

The blood began to pound in his head. Looking around, he saw that most of the patrons had retired for the evening. Only a few piquet players and a drunken couple who had fallen asleep against each other on the sofa remained. Folding the note, he quietly headed to the hall and up the stairs to her room.

"You have a terrible habit of entering without knocking," Miss Sherwood informed him from where she sat without turning to look at him.

Seated at her vanity before a mirror, she continued to brush out her hair. Radcliff had never seen hair such as hers. The curls were tight and full, framing her head on all sides save where a headband secured them from falling into her face. She wore only her undergarments, stockings, and shoes.

"Unlace my stays," she said as she coiled her hair to her neck with one hand, exposing her back.

With more composure than he felt, Radcliff walked over to her and wordlessly did as she bade. When he had loosened the ties, he stepped back and stared at the sensuous curve of her shoulder blades, wondering how she would react if he pressed his mouth between them. The light of the few candles in the otherwise dark room glowed enticingly upon her skin.

She stepped out of her stays and pulled up her skirts. Kicking off a shoe, she propped one foot upon a padded footstool before saying, "Undo my stockings."

It was her gaze as much as the extended leg that almost had him undone, but he knelt down beside her without much expression and reached for her garter. He thought he heard her inhale sharply when his fingers grazed her thigh. His hand was so close to her womanhood. He needed to bend only a little further to be able to look up her petticoats. He breathed in what he could of her.

With a simple release, he untied the garter and gently slid the filmy stocking down her leg and past her toes. He noted they were unpainted. He had expected the toes of a harlot would be painted.

She propped her other leg up before him. He inched the stocking down and could not resist pressing his lips to her inner thigh. As he pulled the stocking down with one hand, he caressed the flesh made bare with the other. He thought he heard her emit something similar to a soft purr, but once he had drawn the stocking off, she moved quickly from him.

He stood to look at her. The stare she fixed upon him had the effect of rooting him to the spot while emboldening him at the same time. He watched as she shed her petticoat and stood only in her shift—a flimsy material in need of repair in certain areas and through which he could see the shadow of her body. He had an urge to rip the garment off her to see what he had only glimpsed for a few seconds the night before.

Standing near the post at one corner of the bed, she lifted her chin—an act that seemed to dare him to approach her. Radcliff needed no encouragement. Shedding his coat, he strode towards her. His body yearned to press itself against her.

"You make it difficult for one to be a gentleman, Miss Sherwood," he said as he looked down at her, his face inches from hers.

"Are you a gentleman?" she challenged.

"In the presence of a proper lady, without question."

"Are you suggesting that I am not a proper lady?"

Radcliff raised an eyebrow. "How many proper ladies do you know invite men to their boudoir and command them to undress them?"

She smiled. "Would you prefer that I were a proper lady?"

Hell, no, was his initial thought as he dropped his gaze away from her eyes and down to her lips, her collarbone, and the tops of her breasts.

"Surely the exalted Baron Broadmoor would not favor a tramp?" she continued. "A harlot? A lowly creature that crawls with its belly to the earth?"

A muscle rippled in his face, and he now felt flushed for another reason. That he had no response for her only made him angry.

"Hang being a gentleman," he said before he cupped the base of her head and forced her lips to his.

This was her aim, he knew. She had won and he succumbed. But he could no longer stave off the painful tightness between his thighs. Every inch of his body cried out for her as he greedily moved his mouth over hers. Her lips hung so sweet and soft beneath his. He delved his tongue into her mouth for a deeper taste.

With his free hand, he grasped a breast through the shift. The heavy orb felt made for his hand. He massaged it with his fingers and brushed a thumb across her nipple. The little nub instantly hardened. He circled his thumb around the pebble while his mouth continued to devour her. He slid the hand away from her breast and down her side to the small of her back. Pulling her to him, he molded his body to hers.

When he felt her kiss him back, his head began to swim. He was about to lose his last shred of propriety and ravish her in a most ungentlemanly manner when he heard her urging him to lie down. Unaccustomed to being told what to do—especially in the midst of lovemaking, Radcliff pulled away to look at her and verify that he had heard correctly.

"Lie down," she repeated as she gently pushed him around the edge of the bed and onto the mattress.

He lay on his back and watched her crawl on top of him. His arousal was throbbing like never before. He grabbed both her breasts as she reached above his head and kissed them through her last article of clothing. He circled his tongue around one nipple. She jerked slightly at the touch. If she didn't remove her shift soon, he was going to rip it from her.

He was about to pull the neckline of the shift down past one breast when she grabbed his hand away and pulled it past his head. She snapped something about his wrist. When he looked up to see what she had done, she had pulled his other arm up and done the same.

Shackles! The woman had shackles attached to the posts on the bed. Radcliff pulled at the binds. They rattled but remained in place. By the time he looked back at her, she had already undone his cravat with a speed that would have astounded Beau Brummel's valet.

"I believe one good turn deserves another," she told him with a small mischievous smile as she began to slowly unbutton his shirt.

Radcliff was still too stunned to respond. What did this woman intend to do to him? he wondered as he watched her lower her head over his chest. She blew lightly upon a nipple before licking it. His erection sprang back to attention. She swirled her tongue against the nipple and blew at it once more. The moisture cooled against her breath and hardened it.

She ran her tongue back and forth against the nipple, pressed her mouth around it and sucked. Radcliff groaned. His nipple had never received so much attention before. He closed his eyes but they flew open an instant later when he felt her pulling at his nipple with her teeth. His groan was now of a different nature as she alternated between caressing the nipple with her tongue and biting it.

He wanted her to stop—and didn't. To his surprise, he found the flashes of pain arousing.

She had managed to unbutton his trousers during this time, and

Radcliff felt a surge of desire and relief when she pulled out his length and fingered it lightly before fisting it in her hand. Radcliff would have doubled over if he were not lying down. He pulled at the shackles to no avail.

Fear suddenly gripped him. He was at her mercy and vulnerable in a way he had never thought to be. He could have misjudged her character completely. She could exact a most terrible revenge with him in such a defenseless position. What if she were mad enough to do it?

But his fear was quickly replaced by arousal when she pressed her tongue against his shaft. She slid her tongue up and down his length and over the tip. When at last she encased him entirely in her mouth, he felt that it might even be worth the prospect of castration to be able to spend inside of her.

It felt extraordinary to have her warm wet mouth about him. He could not resist lifting his hips to push himself further into her mouth, but she pulled away.

"Release me," Radcliff said. "Release me. I shall make it worth your while."

"There is nothing you can offer me worth my while," she replied with an edge.

"If I recall, you were not adverse to my touch last night."

His response seemed to unsettle her. She pressed her lips together. "I give the commands here."

She grabbed him harshly. Radcliff grunted. He looked at her, willing her to read his mind: when she was done, he was going to repay her in kind—with interest.

"If this is how you treat all your lovers, I wonder that they remain such devoted admirers of yours," said Radcliff.

"They always return for more—as will you."

She slid away from him and off the bed. Perplexed, he watched as she strode out of the room. The door to the inner room closed behind her. Where the bloody hell was she going? He heard water being poured. The minutes passed as his body, having been brought to the precipice but not over it, hung in aggravation. Closing his eyes, he cursed. How long did she intend on leaving him here?

When she returned, he saw that her skin was damp, perhaps from a bath. He waited eagerly for her to approach the bed, but instead she reclined herself on the settee and retrieved a book from the end table. His eyes widened in disbelief when he realized she meant to ignore him. The wretched jade!

Forcing down the anger that boiled inside of him, he said, "A work of the Marquis de Sade?"

She gave him a tight smile. "A fair guess. We tramps and harlots do favor the literature of libertines and wantons. I myself prefer the story of Juliette."

He knew she mocked him but could not resist accepting her statement as truth. "The amoral sister. How appropriate."

"Who would not prefer the path of Juliette over that of her sister? Justine strives to be virtuous and is chastised. Vice is rewarded. It is an irony that is all too prevalent in life."

Her last words bore an edge, and her eyes clouded over with a mix of anger and sadness. For a moment, Radcliff forgot his own discomfort and wished he could wipe away her pain. How was it this harlot could provoke such charitable emotions when he ought to feel nothing but disdain and animosity?

He softened his tone, surprising himself. "In yours?"

She looked at him sharply, but he saw the flash of wistfulness before her defenses rose. Her chin lifted in defiance. "Yes. Favorably so."

Her response warned him not to succumb to pity. He had sensed from the beginning that this Miss Sherwood was a proud one, but he saw through her pride.

"You don't believe that—not completely. Or you would not be the daughter of Jonathan Sherwood."

He realized too late that he had gone too far. They were not on such terms for him to utter such a statement, but he could not recall his words, and to explain that he meant no malice— indeed, he perceived Jonathan Sherwood to have been a decent, albeit improvident, fellow—would only worsen the awkwardness.

Her eyes flared with anger. "My father is worth the lot of you."

Silence descended between them. He sank his head into the bed and stared at the ceiling. He was shackled—naked—to a harlot's bed, and yet he felt as if he had wronged her. This was beyond belief.

"Your father was a good man," he commented, wishing he had something more reassuring to say.

"He was," she said defensively.

"Sometimes you can glimpse into a man's soul through his smallest actions," Radcliff prodded. "I did not know your father, but I saw him once, after a poor performance at the gaming tables, give his last shilling to a pauper in the streets."

"Yes, Papa was always generous to a fault."

The sadness in her tone twisted like a knife in his gut.

"And proves the story of Justine," she finished, putting an end to any glimpse of vulnerability.

Radcliff refrained from pointing out that amorality and recklessness were two different qualities.

"Then you are determined to be a Juliette?" he inquired.

This time her smile was wide. Swinging her legs off the settee, she stood and dropped her book. Pulling her shift down her shoulders, she allowed the garment to fall from her body. His arousal sprang to life in an instant at the glory of her nakedness. Her skin was perfect. Not a blemish, a freckle, a vein, or mark could be found. He wondered if the smoothness of it, the relative lack of hair upon her legs, was due to her dark heritage. How she differed in strange but beautiful ways!

"Why not?" she replied as she sauntered toward him. "Would you prefer a Justine?"

The words were stuck in his throat, but he would not have disputed her even if he could speak. With his gaze, he devoured her form, from the downy curls at the apex of her pelvis to her voluptuous areolas. Somewhere in his mind he contemplated the injustice for both the Justines and Juliettes of the world, but he was too consumed with desire to pursue the discussion.

Miss Sherwood, too, seemed to have no interest in further dialogue. She climbed on the bed and knelt before him, flaunting her nudity so close to his body he thought he would go mad if she did not touch him soon.

The last he saw of her was her eyes—was that desire burning in them?—before his vision was taken from him by the neckcloth she tied over his eyes. He could hardly believe it. He had been tied to a bed and was now blindfolded with what was his own cravat. His valet would be shocked wordless to know how the linen was currently being used.

Deprived of his sight, Radcliff felt every inch of his body come to life. He felt her hand brush against his inner thigh and nearly jumped out of his skin. The hand now wrapped itself around his arousal. It did not take long for the ministrations to take effect. He had been close to spending a few minutes ago, and a climax once more quickly loomed for him.

And went.

The hand had ceased its motions. Radcliff could only wonder at what had made her stop. He could hear her breathing, feel the heat of her body near. Why had she changed her mind? He had been so close to spending. He desperately needed her, and only her, to bring him to fulfillment.

After minutes that dragged on like hours and after he began to think that she was going to leave him bound and unfulfilled for the night, he once again began to receive her attentions. She enveloped him with her mouth, taking him so deep he felt her throat. Expertly, she drew her mouth up and down his shaft, wrapping it with her tongue, bringing him again to the brink with ease.

And denial.

Radcliff groaned as he realized at last her designs for the evening. Repeatedly, she brought him close to his climax but never over it. She had an uncanny ability to sense that slim moment right before the ascent to fulfillment. On his fourth time down the dead-end path, he roared in frustration. The pressure was building painfully. Perspiration lined his forehead. His abdominal muscles were sore.

It was the most maddening experience to be so tantalizingly

close to an orgasm always out of his reach. He no longer dared hope nor attempted to will his body to spend. His body belonged to her. And when he came to that conclusion, she finally had mercy upon him and pressed a finger to his perineum. His body exploded in a blinding orgasm that rocked him to the core and jerked so violently he nearly brought the posts of the bed to collapse upon him.

And though he could not see through his blindfold, he could have sworn that her lips curled in a smile.

CHAPTER SIX

⟨⟨

THE SLIVER BETWEEN THE CURTAINS was just wide enough for the sun to slide through onto his eyes. Radcliff awoke to find that he was not in his own bed. Having undergone a marathon of sweet torture, his body felt sore. He had slept as if recovering from an arduous physical task.

Since the shackles had been removed, Radcliff was able to sit up. Looking around himself, he saw that he was alone save for a note beside him. The instructions were simple: he was to return to the gaming hall that evening. Radcliff ran a hand through his hair. He was unlikely to survive many nights if they were all similar to the one he had just experienced.

He wondered many times later that day if he should call Miss Sherwood's bluff. She was no fool, that much he knew. She must realize that she was better off with a cash settlement than the deed to Brayten. He thought about renewing his initial offer of a hundred thousand pounds. If she accepted, they could put an end to this madness between them.

But he didn't.

Instead, he found himself back at Mrs. T's later that evening. He played the part of the dutiful admirer, and once more Miss Sherwood rejected his attentions. This time, however, the note from her was not an invitation upstairs but instructions for him to return tomorrow. He should have been relieved but instead he felt disappointed.

The following evening was more of the same. It was becoming

difficult to watch her flirtations with all the other men. The more he saw of her, the more he wanted to be with her—even if it meant enduring another night like his first. But Miss Sherwood proved more evasive every successive night.

"Wooing her won't get you Brayten," one gentleman said as Radcliff attempted to distract himself with a game of whist. "Have you offered her money in exchange for your cousin's property?"

What a novel idea, Radcliff thought to himself sarcastically but responded with "Who said I was attempting to retrieve Brayten?"

"Indeed," acknowledged another player at the table. "Miss Sherwood needs no such adornment to entice, eh?"

Radcliff looked over at the faro table where Miss Sherwood stood with her usual throng of players and admirers. He clenched his jaw upon seeing one of the gamers attempt to place his hand about her waist. Miss Sherwood firmly pushed the hand away but much more nicely than Radcliff would have if he had been standing next to the man.

"I think Miss Sherwood may favor me with her attentions tonight," said the man seated next to Radcliff at the whist table.

The hairs on the back of Radcliff's neck stood up. He looked sharply at the man and found it hard that Miss Sherwood would want to be with the dandy.

"Told me yesterday that I should have the honor of dining with her today," continued the dandy as he stroked the billowing white waterfalls that served as his cravat.

"Care to wager that privilege for fifty guineas?" Radcliff asked.

"Not at all. Guineas can be won any day, but a moment in Miss Sherwood's company is not as easily had."

Radcliff did not pursue the matter, and they continued their round of whist betting only guineas. In each new round, however, Radcliff raised the ante. Whist was not a game he played as often, but Lady Luck was favoring him tonight. Soon the dandy was down to his final guinea, having lost three hundred to Radcliff. After dabbing a lace handkerchief to his brow, the dandy agreed to wager his dinner with Miss Sherwood.

As she had promised, Miss Sherwood later accepted the arm

of the dandy to the dining hall. Radcliff watched them leave the gaming hall together and waited a few minutes before following. He found them seated at a table in the more remote part of the room.

"These are the buckles favored by all the pinks of the ton..." the dandy was explaining to Miss Sherwood.

Radcliff approached the table and bowed politely. "May I have the pleasure of dining at your table?"

"I fear there is only room enough for two," answered Miss Sherwood with equal politeness.

"Then pray take my seat, sir," offered the dandy. He rose to his feet and apologized, "Miss Sherwood, I beg your pardon and hope, if I may dare, that we renew our conversation. Perhaps tomorrow?"

Miss Sherwood frowned as she watched Radcliff take the place of her prior dining partner. "Tomorrow is spoken for."

Sighing, the dandy left the two alone.

"Did you threaten him?" she asked, arching a brow.

"Not at all," Radcliff replied. "He surrendered the privilege in a hand of whist."

"I shall henceforth not make the mistake of promising anyone such a privilege in advance."

"That will not be necessary. How long do you think you can keep up this charade, Miss Sherwood? Have you not made a sufficient fool of me?"

"I have only begun to repay the favor you provided my family," she answered grimly before putting a fork and knife into the steak that had been served her.

Radcliff felt a desire to pursue the matter with her, but decided that discussing what was clearly a painful history would only anger her further, and he had no wish to infuriate her more. Quite the opposite. No matter how justified he felt in doing what he had done with Priscilla and Edward, he wished somehow that it were less painful for her.

"You have taken the place of your father," he realized as he studied the way she kept her shoulders proud and straight. "You are the head of your family. The provider."

"My father had no sons."

"It is no small role to fill."

For a brief second, he thought she might let down her guard, but she did not.

"My father was not the most adept at providing," she pointed out.

"But he has your respect nonetheless—and abiding love."

She swallowed even though she had not taken a bite of food.

"You were close to your father, I take it?" he continued.

"How do you know?"

"I noticed the other evening you wear a locket bearing his initials about your ankle—an uncommon place for such a bracelet."

Miss Sherwood blushed. "I wear it there that I might resist the urge to wager it if I should find myself in a desperate situation."

"I wish I had had such a connection with my father. I knew little of mine, but he was not the munificent sort. My father spent most of his time in London while my mother and the children stayed at the seat."

"Do you have brothers and sisters then?"

"I have one sister. She is married to a Count and has two children. They prefer the country this time of year."

"How old are the children?"

"The boy is five and the girl two."

"Five? That is the same age as my nephew Nathan."

Her face brightened as she spoke about her nephew. Radcliff was content to let her speak, enjoying the affectionate and animated way in which she relayed all of Nathan's escapades and attempts to be a good person.

"He is five, but seems much older in so many ways," she sighed as she finished the last mouthful of steak.

Radcliff stared at the empty plate in some astonishment. She followed his gaze and grinned.

"I am not the sort of delicate woman who eats only small birds and sweetmeats," she explained. "I prefer a good cut of beef-steak at any time."

Radcliff returned her grin. "I must admit I have never found beef-steak quite so sensuous."

"You should watch me eat an orange," she returned playfully.

"Broadmoor! By Jove, are you, too, a fan of Mrs. T's these days?"

Stemming an urge to glare at whoever was interrupting this rare moment between him and Miss Sherwood, Radcliff looked up to find the cousin of his mistress approaching.

"Penelope was remarking to me yesterday how she has not had a visit from you in over a fortnight," Alastair Robbins continued. "Says she is beginning to feel more like a wife than a mistress. Ah, Miss Sherwood, beggin' your pardon."

Alastair's surprise was poorly feigned. Radcliff knew the remarks were purposeful. It had once been rumored that Penelope and Alastair were lovers when Penelope's husband was still alive. Despite her current situation with Broadmoor, Alastair never wavered in his loyalty to her.

"Not at all," said Miss Sherwood as she rose. "We were finished. Gentleman, I must return and preside over the faro table at this time. No need to escort me."

"Has you on a short leash on account of Edward, eh?" Alastair asked as they both watched her leave. "Pity your fate lies in the hands of one such as her."

Radcliff stood, towering over the shorter man, and fixed a cold stare down at Alastair.

"It is a leash no shorter than the one Penelope keeps about you," Radcliff said before taking his own leave.

The mention of his mistress had no doubt ruined any chance he had of receiving an invitation upstairs from Miss Sherwood. For the rest of the night, she did not even glance in his direction once. That she seemed to only favor the company of her friend Wyndham was no consolation, even though Radcliff had the suspicion that young Wyndham was more interested in men than the fair sex.

After losing a few rounds at hazard, Radcliff went to collect his hat and gloves, thinking he should have gone home hours ago, when the page handed him a note. It was from Miss Sherwood.

When he refolded the note, he looked up to see the page grinning from ear to ear. The young man was clearly aware of what the contents of the note implied.

"If you please, you may follow me, m'lord," said the page.

Radcliff followed the young man to Miss Sherwood's room, though he knew full well its location after having bribed a serving maid—one that clearly had no love lost towards Miss Sherwood—that first night. He tipped the page, half wondering if the lad would return to pin an ear to the door.

Miss Sherwood entered some twenty minutes later. She spared him only a wordless glance before turning her back to him.

"Unbutton my gown," she directed.

He crossed over to her and did as told. Once enough buttons were undone, he slid the short sleeves over her shoulders, caressing her smooth skin along the way. The gown fell to the floor.

He stared at one of the exposed shoulders with a desire to press his mouth there. "There is little between—"

Why he felt the need to explain his situation with his mistress was unclear to him, but Miss Sherwood spun around to place a finger to his mouth.

"Did I give you leave to speak?"

His hunger for her flared, and he moved to grab her to him, but she pushed against his chest.

"Undress me first," she commanded.

Forced to delay his lust, he untied her stays and removed her hosiery, noting once again the small golden locket about her ankle. This time he removed her shift as well to reveal her body. His breath stopped as he gazed upon her glorious nakedness. There was so much to feast his eyes upon: her full and rounded breasts, the voluptuous swell of her hips, a curved and lofty ass, and thighs that begged him to sink his mouth into.

Sensing his appreciation, Miss Sherwood turned to allow him a complete view of her. Once more he reached for her, but she stopped him again to relieve him of his own clothes. When she untied his cravat, Radcliff hoped that she would not use it upon him. It would have been cruel to deprive him of his sight of her now. It was hard enough watching her undress him without being able to touch her.

She tossed his coat, cravat and shirt to the floor, then pushed him into a chair to assist him with his boots. His arousal sprang at her when she pulled down his trousers. Stepping away from him, she reached over to retrieve a bottle from her chest of drawers. He shivered and watched her pour a clear liquid from the bottle onto her palms. She rubbed it into his shaft gently and thoroughly. He groaned, sinking into the waves of pleasure that her ministrations sent through him.

When she was done, she climbed on top of him and unloosened her hair. Placing her mouth an inch from his, she whispered, "Now you may ravage me."

It was the moment he had been waiting for. He grabbed her ribcage and brought her breasts to his mouth. He had never seen such tantalizingly large and dark areolas. He sucked a nipple and felt her arch her back towards him. She circled a hand to the back of his head and pushed his face further into her bosom. Alternating between his tongue and his mouth, he drew long lingering moans from her.

Her reactions flamed his desire, and Radcliff wondered how long he could possibly wait before shoving himself into her. He slid his forefinger to her most sensitive spot, rubbing it till it swelled twice in size. He could feel her dampness on his legs and moved the finger between her legs, pressing into her. The soft moist flesh that enveloped his finger made his head swim. He watched her close her eyes and lean her head back as he fingered her.

He moved both hands to her hips. He could wait no longer. He lifted her above his erection and pushed against her. She inhaled sharply at the initial contact. He longed to be inside her whole, but despite the aching of his arms, he held her and gradually eased her inch by inch onto his throbbing member.

The feel of her exceeded all expectations. This was where he was meant to be: buried in her wet warmth.

She ground her hips against him, but the limited space of the chair did not allow for easy movement. Her legs were already pinned tightly between him and the sides of the chair. Radcliff assisted by holding her in mid-air while thrusting his own hips upward, first with lingering control, then faster as he saw her orgasm begin to build. Her muscles clenched against him, and she bucked against him rapidly until a cry escaped her lips and her body shook from head to toe. She slumped against him to catch her breath.

Radcliff continued to push into her, expecting his own release to follow. But he failed to spend.

She chanced to look up at him, and he thought her saw a mischievous gleam in her eyes. She climbed off him and led her to the bed. Radcliff did not want to wait and see if she would once again shackle him to the posts. He pushed her down and pinned her body to the bed with his own. There was no way he was going to allow her a repeat of the other evening.

He kissed her neck before claiming her mouth with his own. The softness of her lips, the taste of her palatte, the give of her tongue were almost as intoxicating as her womanhood about his erection. As he searched every inch of her mouth with his tongue, he felt her hips once again move towards him. She was becoming aroused once more.

This time he glided himself into her in one motion. One hand went to caress the smoothness of the thigh wrapped around him. The other cupped the back of her head and held it in place for him to kiss. Their bodies ground against each other in strong full motions that rocked the bed and made it cry out as loudly as she. The spasming of her body told Radcliff that she had spent once more.

But no matter how hard he pushed himself into her or how fast, he could not commit his body to spend. He was wondering if he suffered from some form of impotence—nothing would surprise him when it came to Darcy Sherwood—when he recalled the lubricant she had applied earlier. Propping himself on his elbows, he looked into her eyes and understood.

"You wicked harlot," he said hoarsely and pulled out of her to examine his shaft. It was still as hard as when he first began.

"If you are done..." she responded as she rolled onto her side as if to get out of bed.

"Hardly, Miss Sherwood."

He grabbed her ankle, turning her onto her stomach, and pulled her towards him until her ass hung over the edge of the bed. He speared himself into her. She wiggled against him, in defiance or desire he could not tell but no longer cared. It was no longer about her but about his own selfish fulfillment. He thrust himself against her with a rage that made her body bounce off the bed. She was not long before spending for the third time.

No matter how hard he tried, he could not reach his own climax. He was on a hill, always near the peak, but unable to surmount it. Miss Sherwood, on the other hand, spent a fourth and fifth time before her body became limp.

Bathed in sweat, his limbs sore beyond belief, with dawn peering in between the curtains, Radcliff at last spent himself in a climax that was nearly as painful as it was satisfying. No bout of pugilism could compare with what he had just endured. Rolling off of her, he lay in bed on his back and cursed the day he met Darcy Sherwood.

☙

LADY ANNE HAD BARELY SET foot in Radcliff's study before the words tumbled from her mouth. "Have you retrieved Brayten yet from that wicked harlot?"

The English setter resting at Radcliff's feet rose to all fours and growled at the intrusion. Radcliff glanced at his butler, who had come in behind the woman and looked on helplessly. He watched Edward saunter in and settle himself on the sofa. After dismissing his servant, Broadmoor went over the sideboard and poured a glass of sherry. He wordlessly offered it to his aunt.

It seemed to fluster her more. Ignoring the glass, she proceeded to say, "Well, have you? I have not had a decent moment's rest, I tell you. My nerves have been taxed beyond what any woman can bear. I fail to understand why it has taken this long."

"I'll take a glass," offered Edward.

Giving the glass to his cousin, Radcliff made his way back to his chair at a maddeningly calm pace. He rarely had much patience for Anne. The way she endlessly ran her long strands of pearls through her fingers grated on his nerves.

"You do not need to understand," he told her. "Suffice it that I will obtain Brayten."

"Is there no way to throw that wench in gaol? How satisfying it would be to see her rot in Fleet, though it were not a sufficient hell for the likes of her."

Radcliff stilled a desire to defend Miss Sherwood. "I cannot say *when* Brayten will be back safely in our hands, only that it *will*. And if that is all you came to inquire of, I bid you good day."

Anne stared helplessly at Radcliff. "But I—the—well! Only take care, Radcliff, that she does not cast her spell upon *you*."

With pearls flying, she whirled on her heels and left the study. Edward drew up alongside Radcliff.

"Mama would have been far worse had she heard the rumors that I have heard," said Edward.

"And what have you heard?" asked Radcliff, returning his attention to the documents at his writing table.

"That you are consorting with Miss Sherwood."

"Indeed?"

"Come, come, cousin! You may speak plain to me. I know the charms of Miss Sherwood. I heard tell that she is more fun to bed than a whore. Perhaps I chose the wrong sister."

"And how does Miss Priscilla compare in that regard?" Radcliff confronted.

Edward colored. "I—we never—I can only conjecture. There are not the same rumors regarding Miss Priscilla. I had best tend to Mama."

Radcliff watched Edward leave with misgiving. He rubbed between the ears of his dog when the butler entered again.

"What is it, Gibbons?" asked Radcliff without looking up.

"My lord, a Mr. Wempole is here. He says you had requested his presence."

Radcliff stopped writing and nodded for Gibbons to show the gentleman in. Mr. Wempole nervously fingered his hat as he entered. He was a portly fellow with a pleasant smile and spectacles that made him appear antiquated. Not exactly how Radcliff imagined a banker to look. Nonetheless, Mr. Wempole was the man he had longed to see.

The tables were about to be turned on Miss Darcy Sherwood.

CHAPTER SEVEN

᷍

"HAVE YOU EXCHANGED BRAYTEN YET?" Priscilla asked Darcy as the sisters sat over the dining table reviewing the pile of bills.

"I mean to make the Barringtons suffer a little longer," said Darcy.

"But we need the money now, do we not? One of our accounts actually sent a collector to our door. The man said if we did not make payment, he would have to take possession of our furniture."

Darcy bit her bottom lip. "Perhaps I can apply to Mr. Wempole for another note. I do not think he would refuse as we would be able to repay it as soon as we return the deed to Edward."

Priscilla nodded. "If you think it best, Darcy. I only wish there was something I could do to assist the situation. But I fear I only make it worse. I allowed Mama to convince me to buy new clothes for Nathan as he has grown yet again these past few months. Nathan would much rather wear his old clothes and have the money go towards buying a dog."

"Of course." Darcy smiled and put a hand on Priscilla. "How many times have I told you not to worry? We will be much better situated soon."

Though their debt continued to mount, Darcy did feel confident that their financial woes would be at an end. She had simply to see through her plan with Radcliff and in a few months, she would have had her revenge upon the Barringtons and procured an income from their family to boot.

And then there was the unexpected pleasure of taking the Baron. Of dominating him. By the wonder she had seen in his eyes, he was not one accustomed to deferring. The thought of it brought tingling sensations to her toes and warmth to her groin. She could hardly wait to have him in her bed again that evening.

"He hasn't arrived yet," drawled Cavin Richards later that evening at Mrs. T.'s.

"Whoever do you mean?" asked Darcy as she went back to arranging the chips at the faro table.

"Your latest lover."

Darcy looked at Cavin, whose soft golden locks fell across glittering blue eyes. He leaned in towards her, his mouth inches from her neck, and she was reminded of what had attracted her to him before. But if there was one person who numbered as many conquests as she, it was Cavin Richards. And lately, save for Radcliff Barrington, Darcy had had little interest in taking any man to her bed. She could not say why that was—perhaps it was that she finally was settling into spinsterhood—but all prospective amours seemed dreary.

"Why not dispense with the Baron and reacquaint ourselves?" purred Cavin.

"I doubt Miss Treadle would approve," responded Darcy, referring to the woman Cavin was most recently taking to bed.

"Does it matter?"

Darcy sighed. That was the difference between her and Cavin now. She *wanted* it to matter. "I know you well, Cavin. You prefer fresh meat. I would be a bore."

She knew that Cavin could charm almost any woman into giving up her first born. Seducing women into his bed was a sport for him. His attention rarely ever endured past a few fortnights.

"I never complained, did I? If I recall, we enjoyed each other quite thoroughly."

He drew her hand to his lips and pressed his mouth to her wrist. Darcy longed for Radcliff Barrington to come.

"We did," Darcy agreed as she withdrew her hand. "I hope you will cherish those memories as I do."

"My dear, you devastate me."

Rising to her feet, Darcy smiled. "You will not lack in women wishing to console you."

Cavin returned her smile. "If you have a change of heart, pray let me know."

As she expected, Cavin did not take long to move on. She saw him cornering one of the serving maids whom Darcy suspected harbored feelings of jealousy towards her for having been one of Cavin's lovers.

When the hours passed long into the night with no sign of the Baron, Darcy gave up on his appearance and retreated to her chambers. She wondered if something had happened to him, then felt perturbed that he might have openly defied her command to attend to her every evening. He had been diligent in his duty till now. Perhaps his mistress had given him an ultimatum.

Darcy decided she did not want to dwell on his mistress, whom she had already learned was a beauty of the first order. A painful sense of jealousy reared when she wondered if Radcliff was the same in bed with Lady Robbins as he was with her.

"How long do you expect to continue playing James Newcastle for a fool?"

Whirling around, Darcy found Radcliff Barrington sitting in the corner chair. *Damn him*, she thought to herself. When was he going to stop surprising her like this?

"As long as he desires it," Darcy responded, folding her arms. Her worry that something might have happened to him was replaced with irritation that he must have witnessed her latest flirtation with James Newcastle. "Not that it is any business of yours."

"Do not mistake me. I have no sympathy for that man," said Radcliff. "Only that it does not please me that he should be so free with his hands upon your body."

"That is not your business either," she said, inwardly pleased that he cared whose hands were upon her. "You have failed your orders, Baron. Your punishment will not be light. You may begin by removing your clothes."

Radcliff stood and stared down at her. "I think not."

Her eyes widened. In addition to disobeying her instructions, he was now openly defying her?

"I said you will remove your clothes," she reiterated.

"I have no desire to remove mine until you have removed yours."

The insolence! thought Darcy. She returned his penetrating stare. "I give the commands, Broadmoor."

"Not any more, Miss Sherwood, and you will henceforth address me appropriately as 'my lord.'"

Taken aback by this unexpected answer, she threw back her head and laughed, then narrowed her eyes. "I will do no such thing."

"You will, Miss Sherwood, and anything else I ask of you."

She watched him withdraw a set of papers and toss it onto a table. "I had a visit from Mr. Wempole, to whom you owed twenty-five thousand pounds. That debt belongs to me now."

She stared at the papers. It couldn't be. And yet she did not think the Baron was given to jesting. Trying to quell the panic lodged in her throat, Darcy said, "Mr. Wempole would not have sold you the promissory notes."

"I fear his bank had made some rather poor investments of late, and he could not carry your debt on his books any longer."

Her legs felt unsteady.

"So you see, my dear Miss Sherwood," Radcliff continued without the slightest hint of leniency in his tone, "it is *you* who will have to remove *your* clothes."

Darcy lifted her chin. "Well played, *Baron*..."

Radcliff raised his eyebrows at her first act of rebellion.

"...we can call an end to my conditions," Darcy continued. "I will exchange the deed to Brayten for the sum of two hundred thousand pounds *and* the notes."

He scoffed. "I have no interest in such an exchange."

"Then I will sell the deed to the highest bidder."

"Who would buy it? No one of circumstance would purchase

a deed won *by a woman* in a game of whist."

"Then my family will happily move into Brayten."

"There would still be the payment of the notes lest you wish to reside in Fleet."

Her heart began to pound at the mention of the debtor's gaol. He wouldn't—would he? She had thought she had seen a kinder side of Radcliff Barrington, one that even seemed responsive to her, but perhaps she had been mistaken. Perhaps it had all been a ruse to buy time. Perhaps he was as arrogant and ruthless as she had first imagined him to be. And now he could revenge himself for what she had made him endure.

His expression was only one of determination. "I suggest you comply or it will be your punishment that will not be light."

With a difficult swallow, Darcy reached behind her dress and attempted to unpin it.

"Do you require assistance, Miss Sherwood?"

"Yes," said Darcy between her teeth.

"'Yes, my lord' would be the proper way to address a baron."

Her anger overtook her fear. She glared at him but managed to spit out the words, "Yes, my lord."

He walked over to her and undid her pins for her, then stepped back and waited for her to bring the gown down. She stood in her undergarments, feeling more naked than she had ever felt.

"Continue," Radcliff instructed.

"I require further assistance...my lord."

He untied her stays. She allowed it to drop to the floor where her dress had already pooled.

"The shift," said Broadmoor. "Rip it."

"What?" exclaimed Darcy.

"I will buy you a new one, but this one you will rip from your body."

Darcy hesitated.

"*Now*, Miss Sherwood."

Biting back a retort, she grabbed the worn fabric and pulled. But it failed to tear.

"Come here," ordered Radcliff after her third failed attempt.

He grabbed the shift near her midsection, twisted it in his fist, and tore it in one easy jerk. She felt the cool air hit her skin as if for the first time and gasped.

Throwing the tattered shift on the floor, Radcliff stood back to survey her, obviously satisfied with what he saw.

"You have seen it all before, *my lord*," Darcy said through gritted teeth.

"You will speak when spoken to, Miss Sherwood."

She glared at him again. "I protest being treated like a child."

He cupped her chin swiftly in his hand and bent his head to look deep into her eyes. "I take it you wish to be punished?"

Her heart was pounding, but the area between her legs had begun throbbing at his nearness.

"Trust me," he said, "I would take great pleasure in providing you the set down you so graciously provided me…"

He moved his hand from her chin and ran his knuckles gently down her throat and past the curve of one breast. After brushing past her navel, he combed the curls at the base of her pelvis with his fingers.

"…and perhaps you will as well."

Darcy shuddered. Her mind shouted at her to regain control of the situation, but her entire body had already become sensitized to his touch.

"Lie down on the bed," Radcliff ordered.

This was not her, Darcy thought to herself as she obeyed word-lessly. The Darcy Sherwood she knew never took commands from men—least of all from a Barrington!

But she did not even struggle as he stretched her arms overhead and clasped the shackles about her wrist.

"I have a score to settle with you, Miss Sherwood."

She watched anxiously—and curiously—to see what he would do next. When he spread her legs apart, she softly groaned. Her body screamed for him to touch her in her most private places. He breathed in the scent of her, and she felt a little embarrassed that he must surely have noticed the moisture there. The last thing she wanted was for him to think that she enjoyed his command over her.

But her body was to betray her for it jerked wildly when he ran his tongue along her. Darcy pulled at her chains. She had to do something. She could not allow him to accomplish his objective and achieve mastery over her in this manner.

"Stop!" she exclaimed, bringing her thighs together. "What is it you want?"

With a devilish smile and a gleam in his eyes, he replied, "Payback, my wicked harlot."

"I will make you regret this tenfold," she threatened.

"My dear, you are in no position to do anything except enjoy what I am to do to you."

He untied his cravat and grabbed one of her ankles. She resisted, though she knew it to be futile. He tied one leg to the bedpost and reached for her torn shift to tie the other leg to the other bedpost. She lay, each limb tied to a corner of the bed, splayed for the world to see.

With her thus immobilized, Radcliff returned to his task. Once again he ran his tongue against her. Darcy shivered. He teased her with his tongue, occasionally dipping into her slit to taste the thin honey there, sending waves of pleasure through her. She pushed her groin closer into his face, but he pulled back. The loss of his touch was like the loss of air.

Darcy opened her eyes and looked at him. She supposed he would deny her in the same fashion she had denied him.

It was going to be a long night...

CHAPTER EIGHT

(

D ARCY WATCHED IN DREAD AS the Baron sat himself casually into an armchair that he had pulled to the foot of her bed. She flushed, all too aware of how lewdly she was exposed to view. She had had no compunction the prior night over her nakedness before him, but it was an entirely different matter when she was compelled to be on display for him. He directed a blatant stare between her legs and grinned when he met her gaze.

He held up a book—the one from her end table.

"Robert Owen," he noted of the author and glanced back at her. "A far cry from the works of de Sade."

"Does it surprise you that a harlot should have diverse literary interests?" she asked archly.

"No. It surprises me a harlot spends much time reading at all," he replied blandly.

The slight curl at the corner of his mouth suggested he was jesting with her, but she fumed nonetheless.

"Owen is quite the radical," he continued.

"If by that you mean he possesses compassion for his fellow man, then a radical he is."

"Compassion is requisite to mankind, but his proposed reforms are suspect."

"Of course you would think so. You are not among the unhappily situated poor," she spat, then realized he must have read Owen to have made the statement he did.

He thumbed through the essays and must have found the passage she had marked for he read it aloud. "'Children are, without exception, passive and wonderfully contrived compounds; which, by an accurate previous and subsequent attention, founded on a correct knowledge of the subject, may be formed collectively to have any human character. And although these compounds, like all the other works of nature, possess endless varieties, yet they partake of that plastic quality, which, by perseverance under judicious management, may be ultimately molded into the very image of rational wishes and desires.'"

He tossed the work back onto the table. "Why does that passage interest you?"

"Why are you unbearably meddlesome?" she returned as she tried to devise a way out of her current situation.

As he rose to his feet, he unbuttoned his waistcoat. She shivered, then cursed silently as she realized her body wanted him near. It should not. Not like this.

Shedding his waistcoat, he loosed his cravat as he approached the bed. Visions of his naked form from the night before danced her head. She had enjoyed feasting her eyes on the hard sinews of his arms and legs last night and had intended to caress that expansive chest, those broad shoulders, the tapered hips, the hard arousal. But now she was at his mercy and knew not what he intended.

He sat down on the bed next to her.

"No one has ever called me meddlesome," he contemplated as if her words meant something to him.

"Then perhaps you don't know enough people."

He smiled and raked his gaze over her body. A warmth pulsed between her thighs. She wanted to scream at him to stop looking and either touch her or leave her be.

"Would you believe," he asked, "that if I intrude, it is out of compassion and a desire to see to the welfare of others?"

"Ha! A Barrington has no notion of compassion."

He cupped a breast and she tried her best not to whimper.

"Compassion, Miss Sherwood, would not have dictated what you did to me last night and the night before."

His thumb brushed past her nipple, already hardened from her nakedness. He rolled the nipple between his thumb and forefinger, and despite her best effort to block out the sensation, she could feel herself growing damp. She hoped he would avenge himself by leaving her alone.

"Compassion," he reiterated, "would insist I not tease your body…"

His hand slid down past her belly to cup her between her legs. She stifled a groan when he found her wetness.

"…that I not torment you…"

He began to fondle here there.

"…arouse you…"

He lowered his mouth and took in a breast. She quivered against him.

"…tantalize you…"

Desire built swift and fast within her. She closed her eyes, wanting to sink into the sensations he created, no longer caring that she was not the one in control.

"…but leave you unfulfilled…

He withdrew his touch. Her eyes flew open and she sucked in her breath. Would he do unto her as she had done to him? Would he leave her aroused but deny her relief? Of course he would. She might have done the same.

She watched him rise from the bed, but then he settled himself between her legs. Lowering his head, he tongued her where his hand had been.

I cannot allow myself to be aroused, Darcy thought. But the battle between her mind and her body was a desperate one. He still stroked a lust that the former could not combat. She strained against her bonds. Her release was near.

"Please…" she whispered when he pulled away. "Please…let me spend…."

When he only looked at her expectantly, she added, "…my lord."

He plunged back between her legs. She spent with a new release of wetness, soaking the sheet beneath her. She throbbed in every extremity of her body.

Broadmoor unbuttoned his pants and knelt on top of the bed. He slid into her easily. They groaned in unison.

He lightly kissed her nipples and pulled at them lightly with his mouth as he kneaded a breast with his hand. She returned his caress by pushing her hips up to his. Her motions were limited by her bonds and weariness, but the need to spend again was stronger.

Seeing her struggle against her bonds with renewed vigor, Broadmoor pushed himself deeper and harder into her. Their bodies bucked against each other until she came with an intensity that nearly lifted her off the bed. He followed with his own orgasm, groaning and shuddering on top of her.

After a brief rest, he pulled his weight off her, untied all her bonds and wrapped her in his arms. She settled her face in the crook of his neck and released a contented sigh before the feeling of dread returned.

Damnation. He had shown more compassion than she would have to him.

C

"WHAT DO YOU KNOW OF Robert Owen?" Radcliff asked Lord Pinkerton, a kindly fellow who had been a dear friend of his father's, as they sat in one of the rooms in Brooks's.

"Eh?" Lord Pinkerton returned, having dozed off in his chair near one of the multi-paned windows.

"I procured today a copy of *A New View of Society*," Radcliff explained.

"Don't know much about Owen. Some sort of philanthropist, is he not?"

"Yes."

He had attempted to read the third essay, but could barely finish a paragraph before his thoughts were interrupted by visions of Miss Sherwood. Her body was *incroyable*. Supple in all the right places: the breasts, thighs, and arse. Not at all like the spindled forms of the other women he had bedded. And his body responded to her with disconcerting force. At times, he wondered if he could control himself.

The way she spent was glorious. The way she felt divine. He remembered breathing in her scent as they lay in her bed. She had fallen asleep in his arms, and though her hair was tickling his nose, he had dared not stir for fear that he would rouse her. He had stayed, not wanting to leave. When at last she had rolled away from him—for which his aching arm was grateful—he had shed his clothes and climbed back into bed with her.

In the morning, he had gotten out of bed and picked up the Owen essays. But every time Miss Sherwood stirred in the bed, his arousal perked. He had given up reading and returned to her. When her eyes fluttered open, he rolled on top of her. She did not protest. Quietly, they made love with slow and deliberate motions. Again and again.

She had spent for him several times before protesting that she needed some coffee and breakfast.

And still it was not enough for him.

"Shall we see what fare is being served today?" Lord Pinkerton asked Radcliff.

"Nothing new, I presume," Radcliff answered.

Lord Pinkerton frowned. "Right. I swear I am tempted to join Watier's, though my wife no doubt is pleased the plainness of the meals here keeps this in check."

He patted his ample stomach.

"If you will excuse me," Radcliff said, rising, "I shall pass on the repast."

"Don't blame you. Why the sudden interest in Robert Owen?"

"My character has been called into question by a follower of his."

"Someone dared call into question your character? Who here would do such a bloody thing?"

"She is not a member here."

"She?" Lord Pinkerton's indignation turned into amusement. "How delightful. Do I know her?"

"I think not." Radcliff motioned for the attendant.

"Well then, tell me more about her, lad. I think I should like to know her."

Radcliff hesitated. He had known Lord Pinkerton since he was in leading strings, but he could not bring himself to speak of Miss Sherwood to his friend. In part because he wanted her all to himself. But also because identifying her would place her in too prominent a role in his life. She was far too consequential already.

"She is no one of significance," Radcliff answered as he took his hat and cane from the page.

"No significance?" Lord Pinkerton echoed, pointing to the Owen essays Radcliff held. "As well read as you are, I fair cannot remember when a woman has induced you to read political philosophy."

Miss Sherwood had induced a number of things he had not thought possible, but Radcliff deflected the accusation with one of his own. "I think you know more of this Owen fellow than you let on, Pinkerton."

"A friend of mine wanted me to invest in his mill, New Lanark."

"And have you?"

"I've no interest in mills. Perhaps for the children. I have more of an interest now, I must say."

Radcliff smiled and tipped his hat, then left before his old friend could ask more questions. Though a twinge of guilt tugged at him for not having been completely forthcoming with Pinkerton, he felt invigorated, ready to scale the tallest mountain and ford the widest sea. He had command of the current state of affairs between him and Miss Sherwood. He could force her hand and retrieve Brayten at any moment now, but then he would have no reason to see her. And he had no wish to terminate their association. Not when she had given herself to him as she had the other day. And had done it willingly despite the hostility she clearly bore towards him.

The strength of her hostility disconcerted him. Granted, he had spoken the most unsavory things of her, but he had not anticipated she was the sort to care what a man she barely knew thought of her. A small voice—he knew not from where—women would no doubt call it an instinct—nagged at him whenever he tried to reason what he failed to understand.

When he returned home, he summoned Gibbons. He would silence that nagging voice once and for all.

"Swifter needs a good run to work out his restlessness," Radcliff said as his setter pawed at him.

"Yes, my lord," Gibbons acknowledged. "I shall take him to Hyde Park."

"I've a different park in mind."

Taking the reins of his curricle, Radcliff drove it toward the parish where the Sherwoods lived. He had had his secretary investigate everything there was to know about the Sherwood family from their residence to their creditors. He suspected at this time of day, Miss Sherwood would already be at the gaming hall.

But it was not Miss Sherwood he sought.

He pulled the curricle up before the two-storied abode where the Sherwoods lived.

"Ask for Miss Priscilla," Radcliff informed Gibbons and watched as a maid answered the door from across the street.

Gibbons returned to inform him that none of the family were home. Swifter tugged at his leash, eager to leave.

"We'll wait," Radcliff said.

"Out here, my lord?" Gibbons inquired.

"Yes."

He did not explain to Gibbons that he only wanted to see Miss Priscilla and did not want to risk encountering the elder Sherwood sister. He wanted to see for himself the character of the younger sister, and he sensed too much a protective nature in Miss Sherwood. He predicted she would want to interfere too much.

Luck was with him for after half an hour of waiting, he saw a young woman approaching. A little boy skipped alongside her, tarrying every other step and earning a light admonishment from her not to dawdle. Her eyes had aged, but she was otherwise as lovely as she had been five years ago when Edward had taken a fancy to her. His gaze fell to the boy next, and his heart went cold, the nagging voice that had plagued him triumphant.

Here then was the explanation for Miss Sherwood's hostility towards the Barringtons. The boy was Edward's, plain as day. They shared the same impetuous chin, the same streaks of brown amidst the blond hair, and the same charcoal eyes that signified all the Barrington men. Even Gibbons, who had been with the Barringtons since Radcliff's birth, started at the obvious familiarity.

Radcliff doffed his hat as he approached her from across the street. "Miss Priscilla."

The sun was setting and she did not recognize him at first, but when recognition dawned, she grabbed the boy by the arm and attempted to scurry past him. He blocked her path.

"Miss Priscilla, I mean no harm," he assured her.

"My sister is not here," she replied curtly as the boy looked on with inquisitive eyes.

He noticed she moved to put herself between him and the boy.

"What a marvelous dog!" the boy exclaimed when Swifter came up to meet the newcomers, dragging Gibbons in tow. "Can I pet him?"

"He is friendly," Gibbons responded.

Miss Priscilla looked on helplessly. With the boy consumed by Swifter, Radcliff took his opportunity.

"Edward," Radcliff said to her alone. "The boy is Edward's."

Fear watered her eyes, making her delicate features appear even more fragile. Even so, he needed her to answer him. He waited until, lowering her head, she nodded.

Radcliff took a deep breath. "What's his name?"

"N-Nathan," she murmured.

"And how old is he?"

"Five."

"Does he like to fetch?" Nathan inquired of the dog.

Gibbons nodded, and Nathan went in search of a stick to throw to the dog. Swifter, sensing a potential playmate, followed at his heels.

"He adores dogs," Miss Priscilla explained.

The two Sherwood sisters possessed the same father, but there was little to indicate they were related. One was fair and angelic, the other dark and sultry.

Radcliff watched as Nathan found a stick and threw it for Swifter to catch.

"He needs clothes," he observed of the boy's ill fitting apparel.

"He has clothes," Miss Priscilla furnished.

Ah, there was the similarity, Radcliff noted of her lifted chin and proud tenor.

"Better clothes," Radcliff clarified. "I will have Gibbons take him to the tailor tomorrow."

She shook her head. "We've not the money for a new suit of clothes."

"There is no need for your money."

She furrowed her brow.

"I will take care of it."

She hesitated, "It is kind of you, but—"

"I insist."

"I should consult with Darcy—"

"No. Do not let her know I came to see you."

He could see her perplexed and softened his tone. "Your sister is a proud one. She would not wish to accept a gift from me, but the boy is in need of better attire."

"Yes, alas, it is not for want or attempt that he has not better."

"I know."

A small smile lighted her face at his acknowledgement, and he felt confirmed that he had done right to sever the relationship between her and Edward. Not for Edward's sake. But for hers.

"But he is happy," she informed him. "A better son I could not ask for."

He saw the love in her eyes as she watched her son. "Why did you not come to me?"

"You disapproved of my relationship with Edward from the start."

"True, but I would never have allowed Edward to shirk his responsibility."

She protested that she was quite comfortable with her situation and would not seek Edward's involvement now.

Radcliff offered no comment, but he was not satisfied with how things were.

"Darcy and I have done well enough raising him," Priscilla added.

"That you have," Radcliff conceded. "You and your sister have proven to be remarkably capable women. Nathan appears a healthy and amiable young man. My compliments to you."

"What do you intend with Darcy?"

The question caught him off guard, but he met her gaze. "As long as the deed to Brayten is returned to us, you may rest assured that no harm will come to your sister."

The answer clearly did not mollify her, but she did not pursue the matter further, for the time being.

Nathan, followed by Swifter, ran up to them. "He is a grand animal!"

Radcliff smiled at Nathan. "I can see you're better able to keep up with Swifter than my man Gibbons."

"Indeed, my lord," Gibbons agreed.

Nathan's eyes widened. "Are you a lord, sir?"

"Would you like to take my dog out for his daily constitutionals?" Radcliff offered.

The boy's mouth dropped. "Would I? Every day?"

"Every day."

"Most certainly, your Grace!"

Radcliff refrained from correcting the boy's address. "Gibbons will give you our address. We'll expect you at ten each morning."

"Mother! Mother! Did you hear?" Nathan exclaimed.

"Yes, yes," Miss Priscilla laughed.

He danced away from them in his exuberance. Swifter chased after him, barking.

Radcliff turned back to Priscilla and pulled out his purse. "Here. Take it. Purchase some books for Nathan. A boy his age should be well read. If there is anything else you wish to provide him, you have but to inform me. Only you must promise not to speak a word of this to Dar—to Miss Sherwood."

"But how will I explain the new clothes and books?" Priscilla demanded.

"You are, no doubt, a clever woman and will surely think of a proper response."

She was a charming and refined young woman, Radcliff reflected to himself later after they had bid adieu. He could easily see how Edward had fallen for her, though he himself had initially thought her rather simple and humdrum. She had matured elegantly despite her situation in life.

He, however, preferred the rough edges that the elder Sherwood sister possessed and even her temper for it came from a passion that could burn large and high. Darcy Sherwood was full of contrasting manners. She was exotic, enticing and challenging.

"A nice young man that Nathan Sherwood," Gibbons ventured to say. "He has his father's eyes."

Gibbons had been with the family long enough to have earned the right to speak it. Radcliff ground his jaw as he thought about Edward. He could only imagine how callous his family must have appeared to the Sherwoods. No wonder Darcy Sherwood hated all Barringtons with a vengeance. No wonder she had no desire to return Brayten. And he could not fault her for it.

He wanted to rush over to the gaming hall and apologize to her. On behalf of his family and for his own part. For the harsh words he had spoken of her. He winced recalling all that he had said to her. But he had to proceed with caution. He had no wish to jeopardize what he had with her. He could not yet guess how she would react. Even if he were to apologize, was it too late? Would she able to forgive him?

CHAPTER NINE

❦

"YOU APPEAR PARTICULARLY RADIANT THIS evening, m'dear," complimented Henry to Darcy. "And yet I do not find our divine Baron has arrived yet?"

"He had to tend to an ailing friend," Darcy answered as she prepared a table for faro.

"And you let him?"

"How could I not? I am no ogre. And I no longer hold the trump card—at the moment," Darcy added.

"Are you sure you wish to 'hold the trump card'?"

Darcy lifted her brow, but Henry simply leaned his chair back and threw his legs over the armrest of another chair.

"Come, come, m'dear," he said with a knowing smile, "I fancied beneath your fierce independence and defiance of the world hid a part of you that wished for another to be in control."

She wondered if she should be worried that that was the case. Perhaps it was simply that she was, in effect, the head of the Sherwood household, and it was almost a relief to have someone else take the reins, even if only in her bed chamber. She remembered how safe she had felt in his arms—an ironic sentiment given the pain he had caused her family. How could she feel about him the way that she did?

And when she had woken to find him still in her bed, her heart had leaped. Such emotions boded ill for her, and she was relieved that he would be gone for near a sennight. Her sister, however, was not making it easier. It was as if Priscilla sensed a change and was constantly asking questions about Brayten and the Baron Broadmoor.

"Lord Broadmoor—Edward's cousin—he is a reasonable person, is he not?" Priscilla had asked yesterday.

Darcy had blushed and hoped that Priscilla would mistake it for anger. "I am sure he believes that to be the case."

"I cannot imagine him to be as disapproving as some have described."

"Only time will tell," Darcy had replied and went to sit by Nathan to avoid further questioning.

"The dog is an English setter," Nathan had informed her.

"What dog?"

"Oh, Aunt Darcy, I met the most kindly old gentleman—his name is Gibbons—and he is a friend of a Duke—and do you know I think I have never met a Duke before? And he agreed to let me walk his dog every day. And I have been reading all about English setters in my new book. Did you know they are among the best bird hunters? And they have wonderful temperaments."

Darcy had turned to Priscilla. "Did you purchase this new book along with these clothes?"

Priscilla had hung her head and nodded.

"Pray do not think that I disapprove. Only perhaps we should wait on any new expenditures until I have successfully exchanged the deed to Brayten."

"I imagine that to be soon?"

It had been Darcy's turn to avoid her sister's gaze. "There is... well, we must first pay off our debts...but I should think soon."

She had wished she could bring herself to explain all to Priscilla, but she had always made an effort to separate her family from her life at the gaming hell. Nothing was going to change that.

Least of all Radcliff Barrington.

"Miss Sherwood, I presume?"

Darcy and Henry glanced up from their cards to see Alastair Robbins standing next to a magnificent redhead.

"Allow me to introduce myself," the redhead said. "I am Lady Penelope Robbins."

ɢ

THE BEAUTIFUL WOMAN WITH PERFECT alabaster skin, thin wide lips painted a vibrant hue, long lush lashes, and soft auburn curls that reflected every ounce of light took a seat at the gaming table. With her slender shoulders and narrow hips, dressed in an evening gown of fine muslin with the most delicate and intricate lace trimmings, she seemed to be everything Darcy wasn't. Lady Robbins also adorned herself with long golden earrings, a stunning emerald broach about her swan-like neck, and an emerald ring that was nearly as large as her necklace.

"A gift," Penelope explained, seeing Darcy's gaze, "from the Baron Broadmoor upon my birthday."

Darcy stiffened her back, but replied with a smile, "It is most exquisite. My compliments to the Baron for his impeccable taste."

"You must be the infamous Miss Sherwood."

Darcy exchanged amused glances with Henry before answering, "I am indeed Miss Sherwood. As to being infamous, I did not think anyone outside these humble walls would know my name."

"You underestimate yourself, Miss Sherwood." Penelope flicked her wrist, one so slender it would rival the circumference of a child's, at her companion. "I think you know my cousin Alastair Robbins. He tells me the tables here are friendly. I enjoy a game of whist from time to time. Would you oblige?"

"Certainly—for the right price. Our bets start at ten quid." Darcy handed the cards to Henry to be shuffled. She had no illusions that Lady Robbins came to play whist, or any other card game for that matter. From the woman's frequent but empty smiles, it was obvious why she was here.

"If you do not mind, I would like Alastair to be my partner. We are so used to playing together, he and I."

Henry gave Darcy an exaggerated sidelong glance—a motion that did not escape the notice of Lady Robbins, who frowned at the attempted mockery regarding her relationship with her cousin.

"You had a sister, did you not, Miss Sherwood?" asked Penelope as the cards were being dealt.

"My sister is alive and well," Darcy answered.

Penelope raised her thin arched brows. "Indeed? That is a relief to hear. Quite often you find women who, well, are removed from society that they fall into the deepest melancholy. I heard not but yesterday of a woman who, tragically, took her own life."

"Our burgundy here is quite a comfort if you should need to drown your sorrows," Darcy said with what was meant to be a sympathetic smile. It required some effort to remain unaffected when she knew that Penelope's questions were not innocent attempts at a *tête-à-tête*.

"How droll you are," said Penelope. "You deal as if you spend a great deal of time at the card tables."

The cards had been dealt quickly but also precisely. Each player had a neat concise pile of cards before them.

"I understand your father also spent a great deal of time at the card tables," Penelope continued.

Darcy looked at the woman sharply but willed herself not to take the bait. "I was barely out of the cradle when my father taught me how to play."

"How commendable, but I must urge you to spend a little more time in society. Surely a beautiful young woman such as yourself cannot hope to always hide in this gaming hall, charming as it is?"

"On the contrary, I prefer it."

"But surely it has been years since your come-out? If you wait too long, you will be a confirmed spinster."

Having won the first trick, Darcy focused on collecting the cards. She had the sense that she and Penelope were two men fencing, using words as their offense and the fan of cards they held before their faces as foils.

"I have no need for marriage," Darcy replied. "To be discreet about one's lovers would be all too tiresome."

"And have you many of them?"

"To have but one would be far too boring, would it not?"

"Too true. The Baron Broadmoor and I pride ourselves on our unabashed frankness with one another. I was beginning to worry that he would not take interest in other women—you see, I am not eager for marriage either—and am relieved that he has found you."

Darcy could feel Henry's gaze upon her, but she kept her own eyes on her cards. She did not want to acknowledge that Penelope, having lost the next trick, had nonetheless scored. They feigned politeness when they really meant to cast daggers at one another, and Darcy found herself wanting to win the game of whist like never before.

"He speaks of you often to me. But I wonder that he has not taken himself to be seen with you in society?" Penelope continued her offensive. "But perhaps we will see you at the ball being given by Lord and Lady Pinkerton this Thursday? All persons of any importance will be there. I know Radcliff mentioned to me that he planned to attend and hoped I would as well. He and I had a wonderful time of it last season. I am sure you would have enjoyed it as well."

Darcy played a card that allowed Henry to win the current trick. She focused her attentions on the game but was not impervious to what Penelope said. It hurt because it was true. She was no doubt a forbidden amour best hidden from public view. Lady Robbins was Broadmoor's legitimate mistress.

"Ours is a simple association," Darcy said, deciding the gloves had come off, "built upon satisfying but meaningless frigging."

Alastair Robbins went blue in the face, and even Henry Windham choked on his breath. A small flush crept up the high-boned cheeks of Penelope, and her eyes flashed with ice.

"If I were to attend the Pinkerton ball," Darcy resumed as she won her third trick, "it would certainly not be for the sake of being seen with Lord Broadmoor. I am sure that you and I, being ladies of experience, have had our share of men with greater wealth or rank?"

There was barely any need to tally the scores, Darcy and Henry having collectively won the vast majority of tricks.

"Well played, Miss Sherwood," said Penelope between closed teeth. "You are not at all the vulgar creature that I have heard people describe you to be. And while polite society may label you and your sister with that horrid word 'tramp,' ours is a kindred philosophy. It is a shame that you will not be attending the Pinkerton ball, but I do hope that we may have the pleasure of each other's company again."

With one final smile, Lady Robbins took her leave on the arm of her cousin. When they had walked out of view, Darcy turned to Henry and said, "Get me an invitation to the Pinkerton ball."

Henry nearly fell of his chair. "But the ball is less than a week away."

"You are the Viscount Wyndham, future Earl of Brent, surely you can devise a way to get me there."

"Even if I could, why would you wish to attend? It will be a deadly dull affair. Don't tell me that silly woman has perturbed you?"

"Perhaps if she had not referred to my sister as a tramp…" Darcy returned with anger as she recalled the woman's words and departing smile—a smile so spurious it was almost malicious.

"But, my dear, she fully intended to antagonize you and, apparently, succeeded."

"Harry, you ought to know my temperament. I am not so stalwart as to be impervious to such slanders against my family," responded Darcy, a little exasperated with her friend.

"No," said Henry slowly, "what surprises me is that you seem jealous of Lady Robbins."

Jealous? Was she jealous of Penelope? wondered Darcy. She had never been jealous of a woman before, but she would have to be amazingly dense not to realize that she *was*, in fact, jealous of Penelope Robbins.

"I could be—a little," admitted Darcy, "and who would not? She is beautiful and has such obvious wealth at her disposal."

Henry avoided Darcy's gaze by aimlessly shuffling a deck of cards. "…but that would mean you actually cared for that Barrington fellow."

The realization hit her like a collapsing stone wall. It was worse than finding herself jealous of Lady Robbins.

"Not possible," Darcy said weakly. She recalled how furious he had made her, how she had succumbed to his touch the following day, how the slightest phrase of his could anger her, how maddening the pleasure...how safe she felt in his arms.

"It is merely part of my plan to provide him his set-down," she said. "He may think he holds all the cards, but the odds always favor the house. Will you help me or not, Harry?"

"Of course, my dear," Henry answered, sounding anything but convinced.

𝄆

"THANK YOU, LADY WORTHLEY," DARCY said to the regal woman sitting opposite her in the carriage.

"Not at all, my dear," replied the older woman. "I have no affection for Anne Barrington. She tried to deny my application to Almack's years ago on account of a few soirees I had hosted in which the men and women were free to court whomever they wished. Nor could I deny a request from my grand-nephew."

Henry, seated next to Darcy, smiled with appreciation at his aunt.

"I have heard much of you, but your manners appear to me genteel." Lady Worthley peered at Darcy through the eyepiece she held before her. "And you are ravishing—like Queen Nefertiti or Cleopatra. There is no need to be nervous, my child."

"Is it that apparent?" Darcy asked with a wry smile, suddenly aware that she had been twisting and pulling at her rings and bracelets—baubles that she had borrowed from Lady Worthley and were unaccustomed to wearing.

"You have already set tongues a waggin'. I daresay you are creating a stir to match the tales of Lord Byron and his sister!"

When the carriage pulled up in front of the home of Lord and Lady Pinkerton, Darcy took a deep breath to quell a desire to retreat back to the comfortable familiarity of her gaming hall. It had been years since she had attended a ball of this magnitude. Was this the sort of anxiety that young maidens felt upon having their first introduction at Almack's?

She felt a reassuring squeeze upon her hand from Henry.

"Remember," he said, "you are the infamous Miss Sherwood!"

Darcy laughed and felt a little more emboldened. She was able to enter the vestibule with head held high. She knew her appearance, at least, would not want for anything. Priscilla, more adept at the needle, had assisted her with her gown, spending hours for the past few days altering an old dress and sewing an overlay of gold filigree. At the last moment, Darcy opted for a spray of water that molded the gown to her body.

Mathilda had had her maid apply rollers to set Darcy's hair in larger curls, which was then partially piled atop her head and accented with a simple gold headdress. The only thing that needed to be purchased was a pair of gold sandals—the most lavish article that Darcy had ever bought—and a pair of gloves.

Upon her entrance in the ballroom, Darcy nearly faltered. The room had dozens of the largest chandeliers she had ever seen. The silk wallpaper could hardly be noticed behind the brightness of all the candelabras that adorned its walls. Garlands of flowers had been draped along the length of the room and decorated the marble statues that guarded the entry. She had never seen anything so magnificent, not even in the early days when her father entertained invitations of this pedigree.

What seemed like a collective gasp—of surprise, dismay, and disapproval—met her ears. Darcy reminded herself to breathe and to keep her chin up. She heard Lady Worthley explaining to her host and hostess that her niece was unable to attend and as a result she was pleased to introduce Miss Darcy Sherwood as her companion.

"A pleasure," said Lord Pinkerton, a distinguished gentleman near fifty but whose eyes sparkled like one much younger.

His wife looked on with obvious *dis*pleasure.

After thanking the Pinkertons, Darcy moved into the ballroom, following Lady Worthley and Henry. She tried to ignore the whispers, some spoken in hushed tones and others spoken with deliberate audibility, but began wondering if she had made a mistake in coming. Was it not childish of her to indulge her jealousy of Lady Robbins?

She saw Penelope first and felt a sense of gratification upon seeing the woman's widened eyes. For a moment she did not care how juvenile her motivations in coming might have been.

"Diana, what are you attempting?" pointedly asked a well-dressed woman to Lady Worthley.

Lady Worthley lifted her eyepiece. "Where are your manners, Louisa? Left them at home alone with your son? I don't suppose his bedrest had anything to do with the duel he supposedly was not involved in?"

"She is quite a marvelous woman," Darcy whispered to Henry later while his grandaunt was talking to a friend.

"Yes," Henry acknowledged, "in a duel between her tongue and the sharpest sword available, I would lay odds in her favor!"

While no one else dared address Lady Worthley as Louisa had done, it was clear many were avoiding her.

Darcy could feel the weight of all the stares upon her as if an elephant stood upon her shoulder. Seeing the backs of people's heads as they refused to make eye contact with her was no better. Even the men she recognized—men who tripped over their feet to attend to her at the gaming hall—hesitated to greet her in the presence of their mothers, sisters, and wives.

Sighing inwardly, Darcy again felt it to be a mistake that she had come and put the kindness of Lady Worthley to task. What had she hoped to accomplish? To make Penelope jealous? Surely the silent rebukes that Darcy was being handed would only serve to satisfy Penelope.

Lady Robbins was only part of the reason. It had more to do with Broadmoor. And after all the effort to come, the man was not even here.

"Darling Darcy, what an occasion!" exclaimed Cavin Richards. "I thought you shunned social functions such as this."

Darcy let out a relieved breath. At least there was one person here who seemed delighted to see her. She allowed him to raise her hand to his lips.

"You know each other?" asked Lady Worthley with lifted brow.

"Lady Worthley, it is an honor," returned Cavin with a low bow. "I have heard the most wondrous things of you."

"And I the most scandalous words of you. Now be off with you."

"Only if Darcy promises the first dance to me."

Darcy started. Dancing. Of course there would be dancing. Somehow that fact had escaped her.

"Miss Sherwood has too many admirers to be promising anyone a dance," Lady Worthley answered for Darcy.

"Then perhaps you, Lady Worthley, would do me the honor of taking a turn about the floor with me?" asked Cavin with a disarming grin.

"Hrmph," Lady Worthley responded, though it was clear she was not untouched by Cavin's charms. "It has been ages since I have danced. Make your mischief elsewhere."

"I relent for now," Cavin said, "but you have not seen the last of me."

He gave them a wicked wink before departing.

"That one is trouble," Lady Worthley said to Darcy.

"I know it already," Darcy replied.

Cavin was the least of her worries. It was the dancing that concerned her. It had been ages since she had danced—at least any formal dancing beyond a few twirls about Mrs. T's with partners who were in truth too tipsy to be dancing.

As if reading her mind, Henry said, "I make a poor dance partner."

"You have no need to worry," Darcy assured him, "I have no desire to seek a dance partner. Given the reception I have received this evening, I doubt anyone else will be seeking my hand for a dance."

She hoped she was right.

C

"DIANA WORTHLEY MUST BE MAD as Bedlam bringing that wicked harlot here!" exclaimed Anne Barrington to her nephew.

She had dragged her daughter, Juliana, a young woman who had had her come out the year before, the length of the ballroom to make her displeasure known to Radcliff.

Radcliff had arrived late and missed the dinner, but the topic on everyone's tongue for hours seemed to be Miss Sherwood. Having just returned from Sussex but a few hours earlier, he had had little desire to attend the ball, and only his friendship with Lord Pinkerton obligated him. He had contemplated making a brief stop at Mrs. T's to see Darcy, never imagining that she would be here.

"I knew Diana to indulge that grand-nephew of hers," Anne went on. "You know what they say of *him*."

"The Viscount Wyndham?" asked Juliana. "He is most flawlessly dressed!"

"Juliana! Never you mind that one. Future Earl or not, *I* would never choose to invite him." Anne turned to Radcliff. "What devilry do you think that hussy is about?"

Glancing toward the center of the ballroom where Miss Sherwood was being twirled about by Rutgers, Radcliff replied in a bored tone, "At the moment, dancing."

"She means to insult us further!"

Following her uncle's gaze, Juliana thought aloud, "She looks quite regal."

Radcliff had to agree with Juliana. He had always found that Darcy carried herself with a dignity he had initially interpreted as aloofness, but tonight, perhaps in defiance to all those who would shun her, she walked with an aura of majesty as if she, and not the others, deserved to be here. Only once or twice did he glimpse uncertainty in her eyes.

The first instance was when she faltered in the quadrille. He had noticed no one dared approach her for the first few dance sets and had been tempted himself to ask her for a dance. But he wanted to observe her from afar and determine what her motivation might have been in coming. Was there truth to Anne's concerns?

It was Lord Pinkerton who shocked his guests and paved the way by being the first to ask Darcy for a dance. Darcy had appeared content to simply watch the others dance, but she clearly could not refuse the host. Others followed with their requests.

She was not the best of dancers, Radcliff noticed, and looked, at times, painfully out of practice. The waltz was the worse. She and her partner had to make their way to the outskirts of the masses flying by to collect their footing and regain their position in time to the music. Nonetheless, she remained throughout her movements, as Juliana noted, regal.

Regal and *provocative*. Radcliff did not doubt that half the cocks in the room must have stirred upon seeing her. Even from halfway across the room, he could tell that the outline of her nipples were made visible by the way her dress—she might as well have been naked given the lightness of the material—clung to the contours of her body. His first impulse had been to approach her and cover her with his coat. It disturbed him that so much of her was on display for he had certainly not authorized this show. Her body belonged to him.

"Well, Radcliff?" Anne asked. "What do you mean to do with that hussy?"

Narrowing his eyes at his aunt's imperial demand, Radcliff replied, "Ask her to dance."

CHAPTER TEN

&

WHILE ANNE ATTEMPTED TO DIGEST if his words were in jest, Radcliff bowed to his cousin, and strode over to Darcy. He had had enough of watching other men with their hands upon her.

"I should dearly like to give my feet a rest," Darcy was saying to the assembly of men about her as she sat down next to Lady Worthley, who sat observing the spectacle while fanning herself. "And the waltz is clearly my weakest dance."

"It depends on your partner," Radcliff interjected.

She raised her eyebrows. He could not tell if she was pleased to see him or not.

She shook her head. "No one can make me appear to dance the waltz well."

Ignoring the snickers, he held out his hand and returned, "Prove me wrong."

She looked at his hand and hesitated.

"Miss Sherwood said that she means to rest a while," one of the young men informed.

Radcliff kept his stare trained on her until she met his gaze. It was not a request he had put to her but a command.

With reluctance, she rose to her feet. "Very well. Care to make a wager of it, my lord?"

Her last two words wrenched his insides. He wanted no more than to sweep her off her feet and carry her someplace to ravish her.

Brazen little tart, he thought to himself. Even as she submitted to him, she sought to have the upper hand.

"A hundred guineas," Radcliff proposed. Knowing full well she could not afford such a price, he added, "in exchange for two dances."

She smiled in triumph. "Done. You part with your money too easily, Baron."

"Who will judge the winner?" one of the young men asked.

Radcliff stared hard at Darcy. "Anyone you please, Miss Sherwood."

His confidence jolted her. She could easily have selected from the eager men who would have liked nothing less than to see Radcliff fail, but her sense of fair play compelled her to turn to Lady Worthley.

The woman's gaze landed on Radcliff, and he felt a strong sense of disapproval from those mature eyes.

"Very well," Lady Worthley assented. "You best be off for the music has begun."

He led Darcy to the dance floor and encircled her waist without ceremony. She would see that she belonged in his arms and his alone.

She resisted when he pulled her body close enough to his that her nipples grazed his chest.

"Surely this is not an effective position?" she hissed.

"On the contrary, the closer you are to me, the less likely you will step on my feet as you did with the poor lad you danced the first waltz with," he explained. "Step back on your right foot when we start."

Before she had time to respond, he stepped towards her and swept her into the stream of dancers moving clock-wise about the ballroom. The waltz was a difficult dance with women who turned into pudding in a man's arms, but Darcy's rigid frame allowed him to maneuver her easily about the floor.

"Keep your eye to me and not your feet," he instructed, wanting her to relax and relinquish control. "Trust me."

To his surprise, she agreed. Her steps became more fluid and a small smile spread across her face as she began to enjoy the dance. Radcliff smiled in return. The music ended all too soon for him. He did not want to release her from his arms.

"Well, my dears," greeted Lady Worthley when Radcliff had escorted Darcy back to her seat, "this was no easy task you gave me, but I fear, Miss Sherwood, that you owe the Baron two dances."

"Those dances will have to wait," a voice said behind him, "for he is promised to me for a few sets."

Penelope. He felt a possessive hand upon his arm as he turned to his mistress, whom he had near forgotten was even here.

"I beg your pardon for having eluded you the entire evening thus far," Penelope said. "I simply had too many friends to visit with before I could contemplate dancing, but now that I have dispensed of my duties, I am quite at your disposal for the rest of the night."

Radcliff bit back and retort and turned back to Miss Sherwood. But she was gone.

⟨⟨

"HOW CHARITABLE OF YOU TO ask her to dance," Penelope said.

Radcliff barely heard her words as he scanned the crowd and spotted Darcy leaving the ballroom with Lod Wyndham. Why was she always in that man's company?

"But I think it time you bestow some of your generosity else-where," Penelope continued. "It has been weeks since I saw you last—not since the day your aunt paid us a most unexpected visit. I recall we left some business unfinished?"

"Do you mean to tell me that your other lover has not enter-tained you well enough?" Radcliff asked brusquely.

She furrowed her brow into a frown.

"I have known for some time, Penelope," he revealed upon

glimpsing the panic in her eyes.

Penelope laughed nervously. "Well, we are peas in a pod, then? Only your tastes are a bit more peculiar. I could never be as free with my standards…Is it because she holds the deed to your cousin's estate?"

"I see that Cavin Richards is headed our way," Radcliff noted as he disentangled her fingers from his arm. "I am sure he can satisfy your next dance set."

Leaving her to her lover, Radcliff headed in the direction where Darcy and Henry had disappeared. He had always suspected theirs might have been no mere friendship, despite what he had heard of Henry's proclivities. There were certainly those who went with either sex.

The evening being warm, there were many guests who had taken themselves into the dimly lit but well manicured garden. It was a source of pride for Lord Pinkerton, who had imported flora from all parts of the world and retained the garden maze that had been all the rage in the last century. The discreet couples ambled near the steps in plain view of their chaperones. The more mischievous couples ventured into the maze.

Radcliff headed to the maze.

Lord Pinkerton once boasted it could take a novice days to find his or her way out of the intricate shrub-lined alleys, but delights in the form of statues, fountains, and benches greeted almost every turn and dead-end. Radcliff knew his way about only after having spent countless hours in the maze since childhood.

After first encountering one couple giggling behind a bush and another in a quarrel, Radcliff rounded a secluded corner and found Darcy sitting by herself on a bench. She was gazing up at the sky with her back to him. In this part of the maze, only the light of the moon and stars served as illumination. A small breeze moved the faint tendrils of hair at the base of her neck. He was almost reluctant to disturb her peace.

"I hope you did not think you could escape payment?" he asked quietly. "You owe me two dances."

"I never welch on a debt, Baron," she responded without turning around.

He approached her bench. "Where is the future Earl of Brent?"

She shrugged. "In the garden somewhere. What is your interest in him?"

Radcliff pressed his lips together. Her nonchalance was maddening.

"None at all," he replied, "only that I find his manners wanting for leaving a young woman alone in a dark garden."

"Henry and I have been friends since we were children," she said, finally turning to look at him. "He knows that I can fend for myself. I am no helpless maiden."

"Only friends?" Radcliff could not contain the jealousy that crept into his tone.

"Henry was one of the few who cared to be in my company."

The warmth with which she clearly regarded the Viscount both softened Radcliff's feelings toward Henry and enflamed his jealousy. The young man's companionship with Darcy was still far too cozy for comfort.

He sat down next to her on the marble bench, facing the opposite direction. Even with all the flowers in bloom, he could smell the light musk of her perfume. He would have preferred she wore no scent at all for he favored her natural fragrance.

"Still, he should not have left you," Radcliff maintained as he leaned towards her and said in a low voice. "A man could easily come upon you with intents of mischief."

She looked at him with a playful smile. "But then I should scream so that all in the garden would hear me."

Radcliff wrapped a hand about her neck, unable to resist the lure of her. "And by the time anyone could work their way through the maze to aid you, the crime would already have been committed and the assailant fled."

With his thumb, he tilted her chin up towards him. Her eyes seemed to have captured the stars and sparkled their light at him through the darkness.

"What sort of man would have such wicked intentions?" she asked.

"The simplest of men. You look far too ravishing not to be noticed."

He could wait no longer and crushed his lips on top of hers, pulling her to him. It had been too long since last he tasted her. In their days away, any idle moment was filled with thoughts of her. It was as if his desire for her was even greater in absence.

He thought he heard her sigh as he devoured her with his mouth. She gave a muffled protest at his vigor. He wanted to be gentle, but his hunger for her was too great. She could not tease him with her sensuous attire or by dancing with all those other men and not expect him to claim her in any way his body dictated.

He leaned her back onto the cold marble of the bench and pushed the feeble fabric of her gown down to suckle her breast. The nipple hardened instantly for him. He groped the other breast with his hand and heard her moan. His desire pressed against his pants, seeking to mate with her. Having gone days without her, he feared he would not be able to last long if he did not take her soon.

His hand found the hem of her dress and he followed her leg up towards her womanhood. She was wet. So deliciously wet.

After teasing her clitoris until her breath became an uneasy pant, he pushed himself off her to remove his coat. He would have preferred to remove his cravat and shirt if he could, but it would take too long to reassemble his attire.

With her head hanging off the marble bench, her back arched, and one knee pointed towards the sky, Darcy looked like a virginal sacrifice in a pagan ritual. He pressed his mouth into the stretch of her neck and then down into the crevice of her collarbone. He had already pulled his eager erection from his pants and positioned himself on top of her.

He plunged into her, and the bliss that greeted him was like the first taste of food for someone who had been fasting a fortnight. He was meant to be here. With her. In her softness, her wetness, her warmth.

The sound of voices startled her and she raised her head to look at him with nervous eyes.

"We will be discovered here," she whispered and attempted to push him off her.

"Unlikely," he responded without moving. "This is no easy part of the maze to reach. I wonder how you managed to discover it."

"Yes, if I can find it, then others may as well." Again, she tried to free herself from under him.

"Then let them." He stroked in and out of her.

She glared at him. "That may be well for you, but I have no intention of insulting our hosts, especially given that I had not formally received an invitation."

"Then why did you come?" he asked in earnest.

She smiled wryly. "Your mistress advised me that it was an event not to be missed."

For a moment, Radcliff paused. So Penelope had been to see Darcy. He should not have been surprised. Perhaps he should have ended his relationship with Lady Robbins as he had thought to do many times before he had even met Darcy.

"What else did she advise you?"

"I ought not betray a confidence shared in sisterhood."

He could not tell if she was being coy or truthful. He thought he detected a hurt tone, and her renewed struggles seemed almost angry.

"Let me go," she demanded.

"No," he refused and moved once more against her in a motion that enabled his arousal to graze the bottom of her engorged pleasure bud. "I have been without you for days and as sure as hell have no intention of stopping now."

Letting out a cry of frustration, she hit him on the upper arm and strained against his chest. The wriggling of her body beneath his only served to arouse him more. Grabbing her wrists in one hand, he locked them underneath her head and thrust further into her. He bucked his hips against hers until he could no longer tell if she writhed in protest or pleasure.

Her moaning signaled that her resistance had been replaced with desire. She cried out in ecstasy this time, her body shuddering against his. Only then did Radcliff give in to his own climactic end. Grunting low, he shoved himself into her, spilling his seed deep in her womb in what felt like a dozen waves.

He felt like collapsing atop her but knew that her neck and arms must have been sore from her precarious position. He gently pulled her on top of him to the ground and allowed her to rest her head upon his chest. Her eyes were closed and her breath had returned to a more moderate rhythm. Both the feel and sound of her breathing had a calming effect on him, and he felt a tremendous sense of peace.

As he massaged the back of her neck and stared up into the night sky, he wondered if he could ever let her go.

❦

RADCLIFF HELPED DARCY FIX HER gown and her hair so that only the most detailed scrutiny would tell that she had been mussed. Women always bore the greater vestige of coupling, and as he gently cleansed her thighs at the fountain, he felt desire stirring once more. He held back the urge to undo all their efforts and take her again.

"You still owe me two dances," he told her after he had led them out of the maze, marveling at how much more beautiful she looked after being ravished.

"You never said they had to be tonight," she returned playfully.

"Was it not your intention to see me humiliated?"

The words had no sooner left his mouth before he wished he could retract them.

Her eyes were unreadable, but she removed her hand from his and said curtly, "Consider yourself granted a reprieve, Baron."

She returned to the ballroom, leaving Radcliff to curse to himself. He had not meant what he said. True, it had been her purpose to provide him a set-down, but he could have chosen better words. Surely she could see that he could have avoided her the entire evening but chose not only to speak to her but to dance with her—and with the knowledge that he would not only set tongues wagging but had effectively invited upon himself the horrified lamentations of his aunt Anne.

"Quite an engaging creature, I must say," Lord Pinkerton pronounced as he came up behind Radcliff. "Although I can't say I agree with Lady Worthley's contrivance, it is a shame that Miss Sherwood should have been hiding from us all this time."

"She inherited a sizeable debt from Jonathan Sherwood," Radcliff explained, "and attempts to pay it off by working in a gaming hell."

"Jonathan was endowed with a good heart but not much common sense."

"The daughter is a much better gambler."

"So I hear. Won the deed to Brayten from Edward, did she not?" Lord Pinkerton smiled in amusement. "Sorry to say that your cousin had it coming to him."

Radcliff thought of Priscilla though he was sure Lord Pinkerton was not specifically referring to Edward's relationship with her.

"Brayten will be in our hands soon enough," Radcliff assured.

"And do you mean to seduce the deed from Miss Sherwood?"

Radcliff grinned wryly. "Frankly, by any means necessary."

"Miss Sherwood appears a clever girl. Why not simply offer her money in exchange for the deed?"

Pressing his lips into a firm line, Radcliff responded, "Because she means to provide me a set-down first."

"Ahhhh." Lord Pinkerton clasped his hands behind his back and began to amble back towards the ballroom. When he turned to look back at Radcliff, his eyes glimmered with merriment. "Dare say I wouldn't mind receiving a set-down from that one."

Radcliff raised his brows. He had never heard Lord Pinkerton, one of the more devoted husbands of their time, utter anything quite so scandalous.

"If you persist in seducing Miss Sherwood," said Lord Pinkerton, mounting the steps that led back inside, "do try not to do it on my favorite marble bench."

C

THE FOLLOWING DAY RADCLIFF RECEIVED on perfumed floral stationary the directive from Lady Penelope Robbins that he need not visit her anymore. The letter made him want to rush out and see Miss Sherwood. Penelope had done some damage in her visit to Darcy, he was sure of it, though perhaps no more than he had done himself at the Pinkerton ball.

Miss Sherwood had left the ball early with Lady Worthley, to the relief of some and the consternation of others, and left Radcliff no opportunity to amend his earlier words. The ones he had used the day he met her had been particularly harsh, and he winced to simply recall them. He no longer cared what others thought of him if they saw him in her company.

Most of the guests last night were still confused by his actions. Anne had been so befuddled that she did not even bother to approach him. It was fortunate that she did not for he had had no patience for her that night. Edward had simply smirked. Those with cocks understood.

Radcliff could hardly wait till evening to see Darcy. He needed to take his mind off her and decided that riding his horses was just the thing.

Thinking about her, Radcliff urged his horses to a faster clip. His curricle was light and flew along the cobblestones as if the wheels barely touched the road. In his younger days he often engaged in curricle racing, but though he had given up that pastime, he still relished the wind that whipped by when his bays went into full gallop.

Darcy was unlikely to be at Mrs. T's this early in the day, but Radcliff decided to swing his curricle into the area of St. James's nonetheless. As luck would have it, he saw her walking along the alley just south of Pall Mall. She was deep in thought and unaware of his presence until he drew abreast of her.

"Would you care for a lift, Miss Sherwood?" he asked.

She smiled up at him with a warmth that he found gratifying and exhilarating. Her bonnet was a simple straw hat with a white ribbon, but he found it the most charming headdress.

"Are you offering me a choice, my lord?" she returned.

"It is best not to test my charity."

"Very well, then I accept your offer," she replied and allowed him to help her into the curricle.

"A penny for your thoughts?" he said as he led the horses into an easy canter.

She hesitated but then revealed that she had been contemplating a tutor for Nathan. Priscilla had brought up the matter.

"I suppose he is of an age that he should have one," Darcy conceded. "Nathan is quite the avid learner, and there are limits to what Priscilla and I can teach him. And Priscilla insists she has the means to hire a tutor, though I can't imagine that she has the requisite income to pay for one. And we really have no knowledge of where to find a tutor."

"Allow me," said Radcliff, not wanting her to dwell on where Priscilla's new source of funds was coming from or where Priscilla had gotten the idea of hiring a tutor, which he had insisted upon. "I have some experience in the matter, having helped to secure one for my nephew years ago. I know my secretary could recommend a number of individuals of good moral character who would serve not only to provide the proper education for Nathan but also serve as a role model."

"Would you?" she replied with such gratefulness in her eyes that Radcliff suddenly wanted to tell her that he would secure the world for her. "We should be extremely obliged."

"I suppose," she continued with lowered lashes, "there is a price? The deed to Brayten?"

"As I said, do not test my charity, Miss Sherwood," Radcliff said simply.

She looked up at him and seemed about to speak, but said nothing. Radcliff would have given no small sum to hear what she would have said.

"This is not the route to Mrs. T.'s," she observed instead.

"I thought we could take a ride about Hyde Park unless you have more pressing matters."

"That is quite presumptuous of you, my lord."

"I beg your pardon. Have you urgent matters with Mrs. T? Or a poor fool whose pockets you need to relieve?"

"Lady Luck happens to be with you today," she admitted, "but you should not be so bold in the future to think that I have naught but to be at your beck and command."

Radcliff grinned wryly. "Miss Sherwood, I remind you that you *are* at my beck and command, but fear not, for I am confident that you will also *want* to be at my beck and command."

"You are positively the most arrogant man I have ever met," she pronounced, but this time there was no anger behind her voice.

The curricle pulled into the park, and she was soon distracted by the various gazes and arched brows they were drawing from onlookers. Radcliff noticed that whereas other women would have delighted and reveled in being seen in his company, Miss Sherwood seemed ill at ease. She shifted awkwardly and her thigh grazed his.

"Pay no heed to them," he found himself saying sympathetically. "They are fond of exercising their brows."

Miss Sherwood laughed. "Of course. I have lived most of my life not caring a fig for what such people think. I suppose you and I share that much in common."

Broadmoor nodded. "It can be vastly entertaining to test just how high a person's brows can arch."

"Yours went fairly high that day you gave me your first set-down!"

"You mean when you gave me your set-down, madam!"

She laughed again and Broadmoor marveled at how lovely the sound was.

"I had never had my back up in such a manner," Darcy admitted.

"Nor I mine."

She shook her head. "You were abominable."

"And you a wretched jade."

"Yes, only you could make me take pride in such a label. What else had you called me? A Jezebel?"

"Wanton. Brazen." Broadmoor felt his body temperature rise. He had angled the horses toward a small cottage and garden exhibit that had been closed for repair.

He leaped off the curricle and assisted Miss Sherwood to the ground.

"I neglected temptress," he said in a low voice near her ear. He led her through an opening in the fence that led into the garden.

"Yes, many an innocent gentleman has succumbed to my arts," she responded wryly.

"You know I have no desire to be a gentleman with you," Broadmoor said as he pulled her to him roughly once they were hidden from view behind the wisteria bushes.

"How fortunate for me," she murmured as she melted against him and succumbed to his forceful kisses.

He took her mouth in his with a desire to devour her. His veins felt as if they were filled with fire and his erection pressed painfully against his pantaloons. He hungered for her from the depths of his soul.

She reached a hand between his legs and stroked him through the fabric. Broadmoor groaned. He pushed the sleeves of her gown down and pressed his hot lips to her neck, her collarbone, and her bared shoulders. The fabric clung tightly to her and almost ripped in his effort to access her breasts. She gestured that there were buttons at the back, which he quickly undid until the dress pooled at her feet.

Her corset lifted and separated the breasts, but he mashed them together in order to tongue both nipples in quick succession. He heard her moan and felt her body arch towards his mouth. His desire throbbed, but he stalled his need to ravage her and swept her off her feet.

Laying her upon the ground, he pushed away her petticoats and dove between her legs. He breathed in the sweet and savory essence of her womanhood. She shuddered. He put his lips to her clit and bit the nub of flesh before licking it, then sucking it. He ran his tongue along her before pushing into her folds.

He allowed her a moment to relax from her climax as he unbuttoned his pantaloons. She looked at him with a dazed expression but desire burned clearly in those eyes. Even now he found it difficult to look into their brilliance for long. Kneeling before her, he shoved himself into her waiting wetness. Her warmth engulfed him and it took him a moment to prevent himself from spending that instant.

When he had regained control, he pulled himself out and began a slow but steady motion. She lifted her hips to meet each thrust and entwined her fingers in his. Radcliff pushed himself harder and faster into her, her breasts bouncing with each shove. He thrust into her as if he meant to permanently impale her on his erection. Sweat beaded upon his forehead and on his upper lip as he drove himself deep into her. She came with a violent shudder and a scream that could have drawn half the Park visitors.

With a few more quick thrusts, Broadmoor was able to come. Collapsing on top of her, he could feel the points of her nipples pressing hard into his chest. Lifting himself up onto his forearms, he kissed her lightly on her moist brow.

As he looked down at the glow upon her face, he came to the conclusion that he could not be without her.

He wanted her for his own and would claim her as his mistress.

CHAPTER ELEVEN

(

THEY STRODE THROUGH THE PARK and were left alone
for the most part. They talked of family—Darcy was delighted
that Radcliff seemed to take an interest in hearing more about
Nathan. They talked of a great many things: their childhood, pol-
itics, and even the mundane.

Darcy walked with strides light as air. She had not known what
to expect in appearing at the Pinkerton ball last night. She certainly would not have predicted, though she hoped, that Radcliff
would accept being seen in her company. Indeed, he had sought
it by asking her to dance. And though they had not parted last
evening on the best of terms—she later wished she had not been
so easily upset—he had more than compensated for his words by
taking her to the most public of parks.

Scorn and ridicule would undoubtedly be cast upon him, and
Darcy regretted the position she had put him in. His fall from
society's graces would be harder than hers had been for his was a
loftier position to begin with. And yet as she stole a glance at his
handsome profile, he seemed unperturbed by those prospects. His
confidence emboldened her, and her heart filled with a warmth
suspiciously like ...*affection*.

Perhaps she did want to be at his beck and command.

When Radcliff assisted her down off the curricle after returning her to Mrs. T's, Darcy felt another layer of caution melt away.

"I am to meet a friend at Brook's for dinner tonight," Radcliff
informed her as he brought her hand to his lips, "but expect to

see you tomorrow night."

"Very well," Darcy returned, "but do not expect me to leave my position and fall to my knees upon your arrival."

"What an intoxicating vision," he murmured into her hand.

The look in his eyes, as if he meant to devour her, made her flush. She wondered if her appetite for him would ever be satiated.

"Good night, Lord Broadmoor," she said, disengaging her hand before they each found themselves needing to tear the clothes from the other on the front steps of the gaming hall.

He let her go but hesitated to bid adieu. A different countenance came over him—no longer the commanding and haughty Baron Broadmoor. He seemed unsure. She was tempted to reach for his hand. What was it? What did he wish to say?

"I will call upon you tomorrow," he said brusquely, avoiding her lifted brows. He tipped his hat to her, then urged his horses forward.

Puzzled, she watched as the curricle rounded the street corner and disappeared from view. Had she said something she ought not have? They had shared such a lovely evening together. Did he perhaps regret having taken her to such a visible place as Hyde Park? Yes, that must have been it. He had allowed his lust for her to rule over his common sense. Perhaps he was thinking of what the *ton* would say of his being seen with that wicked harlot from the gaming hall.

Her own feelings towards him confounded her. Surely he felt the same regarding his own. With a sigh, she turned to the gaming hall. The evening was much less enticing without the prospect of his presence.

"Darcy! Darcy!"

A feminine form emerged from the dusk.

"Priscilla!" Darcy exclaimed. "Whatever are you doing here?"

Priscilla trembled. "Nathan. He's—he's hurt."

Panic speared through Darcy as terrible images flashed through her mind in the span of seconds. "Hurt? How?"

Her sister's mouth twisted in pain. "A dog. He was—he was

out with Swifter—the dog he has been tending. Swifter got in a brawl with another animal. Nathan tried to intervene. The beast mauled his arm. I swear it looks as if it took his whole arm!"

Darcy grabbed Priscilla by the arms. "Where is he now?"

"At home. Mr. Trevor—the blacksmith, you know—happened to be near and helped me to carry Nathan. The poor thing went unconscious. We stopped the bleeding with bandages, but Mr. Trevor suspects a bone might be broken."

"Have you sent for a doctor?"

"Yes, yes, but we've nothing to pay him. I have but a few guineas in the till."

"Leave that to me. You had best be at Nathan's side."

"Will you not come home then?"

"As much as I would like to, my presence will provide little value. I can do best by ensuring that we have a capable doctor for Nathan."

"If you think it best, Darcy. But Darcy...Darcy, it is horrid!"

"You must have strength, Priscilla! For Nathan's sake."

Priscilla bit her lower lip but nodded. Darcy gave her sister a quick embrace, saw her off in a sedan, then headed into Mrs. T's. How much a doctor would require in payment, she knew not, but she did not intend to return home without some amount to buy time. She went in search of Harry. He would lend her the money if he had any on him. But Harry had yet to arrive for the evening. She asked the page for Mathilda but was informed the proprietress was attending the theater with Mrs. Egan.

"Damn," Darcy swore beneath her breath.

She took her place at the faro table but could not concentrate on the task at hand as she glanced constantly around the room for Harry.

"Have you any notion when Lord Wyndham will arrive?" she asked the page, who shook his head.

She considered borrowing from the house—surely Mathilda would not mind. If she played a few hands and won, she could pay back Mathilda and use the earnings towards the doctor.

But Lady Luck had abandoned her in her time of need. For the first time in many years, the house was down significantly.

"My dear, you are not your customary cheerful self," noted James Newcastle as he took a seat next to her at the card tables.

At last! Darcy thought to herself. Here was a man she could apply her situation to.

"I have in need of some money," she told him. "My nephew has taken ill and will require the care of a doctor."

His beady eyes glowed. "My dear, consider me your savior. There is naught I would deny you."

He took her hand and brushed his lips over it. She tried not to cringe.

"How much do you require?"

"I know not. Perhaps fifty guineas to start."

"It is yours."

Darcy breathed a sigh of relief. "My dear Newcastle, what a blessed man you are!"

"And in exchange…"

His eyes gleamed.

"A kiss?" she offered with a smile, though inside she grimaced.

"I think much more than that is warranted?"

She bit back the retort she wanted to launch at him.

"Perhaps I should apply myself to another," she suggested.

"I think when your situation is known, any number of your admirers would be willing to offer you what you need—for an attractive trade."

"You would take advantage of my need, sir?"

He casually reached into his waistcoat and took out his snuff box. She watched as his fat digits opened the gold plated case and pinched the contents.

"You are a clever woman," he replied, snorting the snuff, "and have long been familiar with the art of the deal."

She rose to her feet, too angry to negotiate further with the man. Whirling about, she again went in search of Harry. She asked the page to send a note to Harry's apartment before returning to the card room. Over and over the cards betrayed her. She owed five songs to Newcastle alone and a kiss each to three different men. At this rate, she would be kissing half the men in London!

Through her desperation, she suddenly remembered the locket about her ankle. For a second, she hesitated. It was the only possession from her father that she still owned.

No! Her father would not have wanted her to keep it if she could assist her family with it. It had only sentimental value, but someone would allow her to use it as ante.

The locket brought her luck at the card tables as she won three hands of brag and had amassed fifteen guineas. She thanked her father silently. It would be one of the few times he had come to their aid where money was concerned, albeit posthumously. She decided to try one last hand. Twenty guineas would be enough until she could borrow from Harry.

She stared at her hand. Two aces and a seven. A middling hand. She eyed the other players. Newcastle did not have a good hand. She could tell by the way he wrinkled his brow. Rutgers was in deep concentration. Perhaps he had a decent but unimpressive hand and attempted to gauge if he should risk a better hand. She decided to stay with her cards.

"Well, Miss Sherwood, you have a flair for risk," Newcastle pronounced as he tossed his useless cards on the table.

Breathing a sigh of relief, she lay down her cards. But a large smile broke over Rutger's face.

"Three of a kind," he declared, showing the four of diamonds, the four of spades, and the four of hearts.

Eagerly he picked up the locket and brought it to his lips. "At last! My most prized winning here at Mrs. T's, I think. It shall bring me great joy when I remember where it once rested."

"Surely you will not stop Lady Luck now?" Darcy prodded hastily.

"Perhaps not, but no one will win this treasure from me!" He deposited the locket into his waistcoat and patted it. "Lest there be a prize more worthwhile than this?"

She rose to her feet and smiled. "But then what would be your incentive to return, I wonder?"

Laughter and a few hollers followed her banter. Excusing herself to tend to her toilette, she went upstairs. Once in her bed chamber, she sank to the floor and drove her fist into a nearby armchair.

She had lost everything: her guineas and her locket. There was nothing left to wager. How was she to help Nathan now? How was she to help any in her family? Would Lady Luck never grace the Sherwoods? Would she only tease them, as she had with the deed to Brayten, only to strip it from them?

The tears began to roll.

"Oh, Papa," she moaned. If only he had been more prudent... but it was not in his nature. He had too much the blithe spirit. She loved and hated him for it.

Come, come, my girl, she rallied herself. Such sentiments did nothing to help Nathan. She had to put her mind to the task at hand.

There was the offer from Newcastle. And he would not be the only one willing to pay for her favors. She would become a true whore. But would she not do anything for Nathan? Of course she would.

Wiping away her tears, she took in a deep breath and prepared herself to return to the card room. She opened the door to find the Baron Broadmoor upon her threshold.

She started, "Lord Broadmoor!"

"Miss Sherwood..." His gaze roved over her features, and he took her by the shoulders. "What is it?"

"What is what?" she returned.

"Something is the matter? What is it?"

Her defenses threatened to crumble at the sound of his concern. How was he able to see her troubles?

He led her back into the room and closed the door after them. "Tell me," he urged.

She couldn't. Could she?

"Tell me," he repeated softly.

The dam gave. She could not hold back the tears. Her strength deserted her and she had to clutch at his arms for support. To her relief, he held her close. Those strong arms seemed able to protect her from anything, and in his compassion, she indulged herself.

"I can help," he said when the brunt of her tears had subsided. "But you must tell me what has happened."

"It is Nathan—he's been hurt—terribly."

She felt his arms stiffen about her.

"Mauled by a dog," she explained between shudders.

His jaw tightened. "Where is he?"

"With my sister. And a doctor—I hope."

"You hope? Has one not been called?"

Swallowing a new wave of sobs threatening to overcome her, she sputtered, "I told Priscilla to send for one, but we have no means to pay for one. I pray that we shall find one with a charitable heart, one who will see that a boy—a child—is in need of aid…surely a doctor will help him even if he cannot be compensated?"

He did not answer her immediately.

"I can come up with the money," she added desperately, "I've been trying…"

He put a finger to his lips. "Worry not. If you will go and tend to Nathan and your sister, I will see to the doctor. Will you do as I say?"

Oddly assured, she found herself nodding.

"Good," he said. "I will send a physician to your address."

He saw her into his chaise.

"Your friend," Darcy remembered. "Were you not to have dinner with a friend?"

"I ate fast."

Before urging his coachman on, he brought her hand to his lips. It was dark, but she could see the look in his eyes. It made her heart soar. He had come to see her because he *wanted* to see her. She marveled that she could feel such happiness even in the midst of distress.

The chaise did not travel fast enough for her. When it came upon the Sherwood residence, she flew into the house and up the stairs.

"Darcy!" Priscilla cried in relief.

Even Leticia proffered a "thank heavens."

Darcy approached the bed where Nathan lay, groaning, his form small, his countenance pale. She would sooner have had a dagger twisted into her belly.

"Where is the doctor?" she whispered to Priscilla.

"He came and went," Priscilla replied. "Said there was little to be done till the bleeding stops. And, Darcy, it won't stop bleeding!"

Mrs. Sherwood paced the floor, wringing her hands and bemoaning the evils of dogs, until Darcy bade her leave the room. The two sisters in silent watch over Nathan until a knock sounded at the front door. Darcy leaped to her feet. Was it Broadmoor?

"Hornsby. Dr. Hornsby, at your service, Miss Sherwood," the gentleman at the door greeted as he removed his hat. "I was sent by Lord Broadmoor."

She closed her eyes and uttered a silent appreciation to the Baron before ushering the doctor to Nathan's room.

"He is fortunate," Dr. Hornsby pronounced to Darcy and Priscilla after examining the boy. They stood in the hall and spoke in hushed tones. "There appear to be no broken bones. I gave him a sedative to make him sleep. When the wounds are better healed, the stitching can be removed."

"But he is at risk of infection," Dr. Hornsby continued. "Change his bandages often and clean the wounds as best you can. Watch for fever. I will be by tomorrow to see how he fares."

Darcy walked the doctor to the door while Priscilla returned to Nathan's bedside. Her sister would no doubt stay the entire night there.

"Doctor Hornsby, how can we thank you for your kindness?" she asked.

"Not at all, my child."

"The fee for your services—"

Dr. Hornsby shook his head. "Let us say I am indebted to Lord Broadmoor and thank you for the chance to repay the favor."

The fever appeared the second day, but true to his word, Dr. Hornsby came every day to see to Nathan and sent a nurse to assist the family. Priscilla and Darcy took turns sitting beside Nathan's bad. Gradually the fever broke, and though weak, Nathan was able to sit up in bed and inquire after Swifter.

Priscilla shook her head. "He worries more for the dog than for himself."

"Someone has to run with Swifter," Nathan protested. "Mama, can you read my letter again?"

Darcy raised her brows inquisitively.

Priscilla held up a parchment and read aloud, "'Dear Master Sherwood, we eagerly await your recovery. Signed, Gibbons and Swifter.'"

Nathan smiled. "Eagerly await."

When Nathan was once again asleep, Darcy urged her sister to rest.

"And you, Darcy? What of you?" Priscilla returned.

"With the nurse here, I ought to return to Mrs. T.'s," Darcy answered. "She is sure to have missed me."

"You are a wonder. How did you ever come across such a wonderful physician?"

"I didn't. Lord Broadmoor..."

"The Baron Broadmoor?"

Darcy relented and confessed that she had told him about Nathan and that he had been the one to send for the doctor.

Priscilla seemed deep in thought.

"Are you troubled by it?" Darcy asked.

"No. I..."

"What is it, Priscilla?"

"Nothing. I am weary and find I cannot think well."

Darcy nodded, but she sensed that her sister wanted to tell her something. She wondered what it could be?

CHAPTER TWELVE

&

"My locket!"

With a wide smile, Broadmoor placed the object in her hands.

"But how did you come by it?" Darcy inquired.

"By no easy means," he replied. "It would have cost me less to procure you a new one."

"And how did you know?"

"Rutgers couldn't stop boasting about it. I overheard him and challenged him to play for it. He didn't want to at first. Had to wager some forty pounds before he would give it over."

In an uncharacteristic show of exuberance, she threw her arms about him. He stumbled backwards, and they both fell onto her bed. Realizing what she had done, she pulled back from him and cast a suspicious eye.

"And what do you wish from me? Forty pounds? The deed to Brayten."

"Good God, woman. Can a charitable deed not go uncensored? It is yours. Free and clear. Though perhaps I will settle for a kiss. Seems only fair since you were giving kisses away to half the men in London the other night."

"Then a kiss, my lord, you shall have."

She rolled back on top of him and pressed her lips down upon his, drawing him into her mouth. His hand went to the back of her head as she showed him the depths of her appreciation, pressing her tongue low into his mouth, engaging his tongue, and caressing his lips.

"Mmmm," he approved when she lifted her head for breath. "Worth every pound."

She stared at him, her heart filled with gratitude.

"What is it?" he asked.

"No one has shown our family such kindness before," she answered.

"You've not needed it." He stroked the hair from her face. "You've been the little father for your family."

She crooked her smile. "Not an effective one. I abhor to think what would have happened to Nathan were it not for Dr. Hornsby."

"Hornsby tells me that Nathan is recovering with astonishing alacrity."

"He couldn't wait to get back to walking Swifter." She shook her head. "I would like nothing more than to give him his own dog."

"You will. You are Darcy Sherwood. Many things are possible with you."

How was it he could have more confidence than she? she wondered.

"Come," he said, "let us return the locket to where it belongs."

He took it from her and sat up to clasp it about her ankle. His hand smoothed over her stocking.

"I think," he said, his hand trailing up to her knee, "I shall require more than a kiss."

"Such as?" she teased.

Bringing her mouth to his, he leaned her back down on the bed, reversing their previous position. She wound her hands around his neck and pressed her body eagerly against him. They kissed with surprising thoroughness, given the frenzied heat that always ruled their bodies when they came into contact. In a slower, scintillating manner, their tongues danced and plumbed the depths of their mouths.

Broadmoor cupped her buttock and fitted his hardness between her legs. She curled a leg about his, willing to delay her need to couple her body to his, as she explored him through his clothes. Her hands went under his coat and up his back. He unlocked his mouth from hers and applied the heat of his mouth to her neck.

"Darcy…" he moaned into her throat as he devoured her, trailing his mouth to the tops of her breasts.

He cupped a breast and pushed it up to his mouth. He pulled the bodice down.

"You have the most marvelous nipples, Miss Sherwood," he told her before his mouth descended upon her.

His attentions upon her breast had the effect of teasing the sex between her legs.

"And you, Lord Broadmoor," she began to say as his erection pressed against her thigh, flaring her carnal hunger.

"Radcliff," he supplied. "I think you and I qualify as being on intimate terms."

"Radcliff, then."

Grinning, she reached for his buttons. She liked the sound and feel of his name upon her mouth. She slid her hand into his pants to grasp his arousal. He grunted his approval and was content for her to play with him a while. When she glanced into his eyes, there seemed more than lust shining there. She herself felt something more intense than desire, a feeling that made her patient, that made her want to savor the moment, to bring him pleasure.

"Too pleasing," he said gruffly, grabbing her hand away from him and pinning it above her head.

"I could take you in many ways," she said. "With my hands—or in my mouth."

He closed his eyes and groaned. "Not tonight, but soon. You cannot proffer such suggestions and not see them through."

Sliding down he lifted her skirts and settled his head between her thighs. She shivered when he licked her there.

"I would enjoy the chance, Lord Broad—Radcliff."

He stroked her with his tongue, fondling her in the most sensitive ways, sending waves of bliss through her belly, and taking her breath away. She cried out as tremors erupted through her. Replacing his tongue with his finger, he pushed the last of her spasms through her. But already a fresh desire had begun to build within her. She reached over and pulled out his shaft, felt the weight of its rigidity.

"Take me, Radcliff," she directed.

He obliged and speared himself into her wetness. Wantonly, she wrapped her legs around him and ground her pelvis at him. He held himself above her, rolling his hips, as he fitted his mouth about her. She kissed him hungrily, carelessly, as she bucked him against him. The insides of her body began to contract tighter and tighter before, like a spring being sprung, it exploded in a euphoric paroxysm. Grunting low in his throat, Radcliff thrust himself deep and spent with her.

Despite the heat of their clothes, they lay in each other's arms. And this, too, was bliss.

"I should return to the card room," Darcy murmured after she had waited as long as she could, wishing they could lay together forever.

"No."

The roughness of his tone startled her. "But they are awaiting my presence."

A cloud seemed to pass over his eyes, and he pressed his lips together firmly, tightening his hold upon her.

"Leave them be. You need not tend to them."

"But I am expected."

"You don't have to be."

"Don't have to be expected?"

He fixed an intense gaze upon her. "Be my mistress."

Darcy blinked a few times. "How many mistresses do you need?"

"Only one. You."

"Do you not have one already?"

"Lady Robbins and I have severed our relationship."

"Ah."

"I would treat you well," he pledged. "You would want for nothing. I can set up an apartment for you, provide you with clothing and servants."

The image of a life of luxury danced before her. One that could surpass the comforts of her life when her father had fared well. But her thoughts quickly turned to Priscilla and Nathan.

"I am comfortable enough residing with Mrs. T," Darcy said, her voice shaking slightly.

"I could secure accommodations for your sister and nephew as well," he disclosed.

Surprised at how well he knew her thoughts, she hesitated.

"You would be an outcast," she demurred while a voice inside her scolded her for being a fool. What idiot would not take his offer?

"Other men have had far more controversial love affairs and survived."

Her heart was pounding in her head. A home for Priscilla and Nathan. Her own living conditions secured. She would no longer have to work at the gaming hall. She could be with *him*.

And yet, she had never been anyone's mistress before. What did a mistress do? What was the appropriate etiquette for a mistress? Her responsibilities? Her freedoms?

Her words to him from what seemed ages ago echoed in her mind: I am no man's mistress. She would be bound to him. Dependent upon him. Her independence gone.

How long before she went the way of Penelope Robbins? Until he found a wife? That she could not handle.

"No," Darcy said, and though she avoided his gaze, she could tell he was surprised.

"That is hardly a rational answer," he responded.

She looked him in the eyes, hoping he did not detect the uncertainty within her. "I am no man's mistress."

"And why is that?" he asked angrily. "Because you wish to entertain the attentions of more than one lover?"

"Because I do not wish to be at any man's beck and command." Sensing his anger growing, she added quickly. "If you please, my lord, Mrs. T is waiting for me."

"It pleases me not at all," he retorted.

But Darcy pretended she did not hear and went to wrap a shawl about herself. He strode over and caught her by the arm.

"Have you nothing else to say?" he asked.

"I have said all that I have to say on the matter."

"But what of…us?"

She was trembling so hard on the inside, she thought she would shatter into pieces, but she mustered a reply. "What about us?"

He paled, but he was not the only one to feel a dagger through the heart.

"I have patrons to attend," she said before fleeing down the stairs.

She almost knocked one of the maidservants over in her haste. She dared not look back.

CHAPTER THIRTEEN

(

"ARE YOU NOT HAVING BREAKFAST, Darcy? You look pale. Are you feeling ill?" inquired Mathilda as she sipped her favorite morning beverage of hot chocolate.

Her lack of appetite could be attributed to the nausea she felt upon waking, but Darcy felt the culprit could equally lie in the restless night she had had. Despite her best attempts to clear her mind, *he* permeated her thoughts like water through a sponge.

Her body felt empty without his touch. When she had thought of how forcefully he had taken her or how tender had been his kiss, her hand had crept to her mons. But even after bringing herself to spend, sleep persisted in eluding her.

"He asked me to be his mistress," Darcy revealed as she stared into her coffee and stirred it for no reason.

"What? His money must make him daft. He suffers delusions if he thinks you would even entertain the notion for the slightest second. Even *I* would not lay with him, and I am nearer his age than you. Only yesterday he had the effrontery to complain to me of his gout…"

"Not James Newcastle. The Baron Broadmoor."

"Oh," Mathilda frowned. "And how did you answer?"

"That I am no man's mistress."

"A sensible answer."

"Then why do I feel as if I have been in error?" Darcy responded, poking at the holes in her crumpet. "No doubt many other women would be delighted to be his mistress."

"Yes, and no doubt they will have their turn," Mathilda stated as she spread more jam on her toast. "You know how men are. It is even worse when they take a wife."

"But Radcliff is no Cavin Richards."

Mathilda raised her eyebrows. "It's 'Radcliff' now, is it? Well, I would agree he differs from a lot of the men here, but why should you give up your freedom and the attentions of many to be devoted to just one?"

Of course Mathilda was biased: she had no interest in losing Darcy. Fear of losing freedom was only partly the answer. Darcy was more concerned with *dignity*. It was true she was a nobody in his world, and yet she could not help but long for more.

"I must say that the amount of time you have spent with him has not been good for business," Mathilda added. "Word has spread that you and Broadmoor are lovers. You know servants can never keep their mouths shut if their lives depended upon it. Only fools like Newcastle remain oblivious. Nonetheless, I should hate to have to find a replacement."

Her words shocked Darcy. Mathilda had never suggested she needed anyone but Darcy. In fact, Mathilda had often remarked that Darcy aged so well that she could work in the gaming hall till she were fifty and still be able to attract men young and old.

There was an edge in Mathilda's tone that Darcy had never heard before. She had noticed that attendance at the gaming hall had dipped somewhat but had not realized it was dramatic enough to concern Mathilda.

"I have been distracted from my occupation," Darcy acknowledged.

"Well, never you mind what has passed. It may be prudent, however, to sever your ties with the Baron."

The mere thought pained her, though she had considered that route herself as she had tossed in her bed last night.

"Afterall," said Mathilda with a mouthful of toast and jam, "it isn't as if you were in love with the fellow."

No, it wasn't, Darcy thought to herself, or was it?

C

THE REALIZATION STRUCK HER WITH all the force of a
battleship in full sail. She *was* in love with Radcliff.

It was absurd. Irrational. Foolish.

And true. Darcy concluded with a heavy heart that Mathilda
was correct. Unless she intended to be his mistress, there was no
reason to continue their affair. It was a path that could only end
in pain and misery. She knew already that she could not bear the
thought of Radcliff with another woman.

Best to move on with their own lives.

Even Henry, more a romantic than she or Mathilda, conceded
that was the wise decision and offered his carriage when Darcy
opted not to wait another day.

"You can't just walk up to his home willy-nilly," Henry
explained. "If you mean to hand a man a rejection, do it bang-up
with *style*."

Radcliff Barrington's residence in Grosvenor Square was a simple but stately Georgian townhouse. When Harry's carriage pulled
up before it, Darcy had to quell her desire to ask the coachman to
turn around and bring her back to Mrs. T's. Instead, she told the
man to wait and mounted the front steps of the house with legs
that felt as unsteady as those of a centurian.

A chary eyed butler greeted her at the door. When she gave
her name and asked for the Baron, the man gave no indication of
surprise or disapproval. Darcy wondered if he would require her
to wait outside the door, but he invited her in and asked that she
wait in the anteroom. He indicated a settee, but Darcy was too
nervous to sit. She distracted herself by examining the pastoral
paintings on the walls.

Perhaps Radcliff would not be in, she thought almost hopefully.
The butler dispelled any reprieve when he returned to announce
that his lordship would see her in the study.

Taking in a deep breath, Darcy followed the butler. The deed
to Brayten was tucked in her sleeve, reminding her that she had
a mission to see through. It would not be easy, but they would all

be better for it upon completion.

Radcliff was standing behind his writing desk. In the comfort of his own home, dressed somewhat informally in a white shirt, satin vest, and beige pants, he seemed to Darcy particularly handsome. She had always liked his sense of fashion—in line with the pinks of the ton but never ostentatious to qualify as a fop.

"Miss Sherwood, to what do I owe this pleasure?" he asked and gestured to a seat.

Darcy shook her head, wishing she could read his emotions. Was he glad that she had come? Displeased? Surprised?

"You plan a short visit, I take it," he noted. "Would you care for a glass of port nonetheless?"

"No, thank you," she answered. "I came to offer the deed to Brayten in exchange for the promissory notes that you hold and a sum of fifty and five thousand pounds."

The words tumbled from her mouth for she feared if she did not speak quickly, the words would catch in her throat and never come out.

"Is that all?"

"It totals the amount that Edward had initially owed."

"Yes, I noticed the tidy sum." He went to the sideboard and poured a glass of wine before turning back to face her. "What if I refuse?"

"Then I will have to turn your family out of Brayten," Darcy responded with difficulty and saw his face cloud over.

"I see."

Watching him speak in such methodical even tones when she felt besieged by all manner of emotions, Darcy almost preferred that he were furious.

"I can offer you much more as my mistress," he said.

"Yes, but I have no interest in being your mistress," she uttered.

"You drive a hard bargain, Miss Sherwood. What is it you want?"

To be yours and yours alone, and for you to be mine and mine alone.

"Would five thousand pounds a year for you and your family suffice?" he pressed.

"And how long would that last, my lord? Until you lost interest in us?" asked Darcy. She shook her head when she saw he meant to protest. "Even if you promised an eternity, I cannot be bought. There is no amount you can name that would induce me to relinquish my freedom."

"You prefer to toil in that gaming hell?" he asked in disbelief.

"I prefer not to have to answer to one man."

His gaze bore into her, and she saw his eyes flame. "Because you favor having more than one lover?"

Darcy wanted to disappear into the earth, but she forced some words from her mouth. "That is a consideration…"

He grabbed her suddenly by the arms with the same intensity he had done the day they met. "Do you mean to say that I am not man enough for you?"

She had never heard such harshness—she would have expected him to want to tear off her head if it were not for the tortured undertones that she could hear beneath the surface of his anger. How she wanted to reassure him that no one made her feel the way he did. Even now all she wanted to do was yield into his embrace, wanted his lips on hers, wanted him inside of her.

But she lowered her gaze away and murmured, "Did you not once call me a harlot, Baron? I did not then nor now dispute—"

Abruptly he let her go and stepped away from her. There was pain in his eyes, and at that moment she would have preferred a dagger in her chest than to see that emotion in him.

"I thought…" he said, his voice hoarse and hollow.

"That you were different? That I was different?" Darcy finished for him. She shook her head and drove the last nail in the coffin. "No, my Baron Broadmoor. Ours was an amusing romp. But my interest now lies in our trade. I believe my offer is more than fair."

She wanted to melt into the center of the earth and disappear. A part of her wanted to assure him that she did not refuse him lightly, but her pride would not allow her to admit that or that she had been hurt by the fact that she could not be more than a mistress to him.

"The fifty-five thousand pounds will have to be paid in installments," he said, pulling the notes from his desk.

She had never heard his voice ring so hollow. "I understand."

"I will work out the terms with my accountant and forward them to you for approval."

"Thank you."

She pulled out the deed to Brayten. Her stepmother had thought it such a blessing, but it had proved a bane. She held it out to Radcliff as she took the promissory notes. His eyes searched her face, but she wanted only to flee from him as soon as possible. They exchanged the parchments, but Darcy felt no gain, only loss.

"Darcy..."

"I bid you good day, Baron," Darcy said quickly over the lump that threatened to cave her throat in. She whirled on her heels and rushed out of Broadmoor House before he could hear the sound of her heart breaking.

☾

"ONLY FIFTY-FIVE THOUSAND POUNDS?" CRIED Mrs. Sherwood. "But Brayten is worth far more than that!"

"Yes, but in our hands it cannot command any sum," Darcy explained as she looked out the kitchen window at the setting sun. She would have to hurry to make it to Mrs. T.'s before nightfall.

"But I had settled on a new apartment for us—one in Berkeley Square."

"Mother!" Priscilla chided as she rinsed the dishes from supper. "Fifty-five thousand pounds is an amount I would never have dared to dream, but we cannot afford such luxuries as living in Berkeley Square. You must rescind the agreement."

"No," said Darcy, siding with her stepmother for the first time. "It is time we sought a better neighborhood for Nathan—and ourselves. Perhaps a small apartment..."

"But we still have other debts to discharge. I was able to hold off the collectors today—they were prepared to take our furniture—only I begged them on whatever kindness existed in them to spare us a few more days."

"And I promised the mantua maker that I would pay her in a timely manner," added Mrs. Sherwood.

"And I suppose there is the matter of the tutor as well," said Darcy. "Nathan seems quite taken with him."

"Yes," said Priscilla. "Mr. Davis told me that Nathan has a mind that seems starved for knowledge for he drinks in whatever his tutor instructs."

"Then we must keep this Mr. Davis. I know not what income you are able to bring in, Priscilla, but I cannot imagine it to be enough to cover the payment of the tutor."

Darcy sat down at the kitchen table as she tried to add up all the expenses. She felt weak and had not slept well since her visit to Broadmoor House.

"Are you feeling ill?" Priscilla asked. "You look pale."

"Yester night was long," answered Darcy dismissively.

"Will you have to return to Mrs. T's tonight?"

"Nathan will require more than what Brayten has procured for us. I want the best for him. I wish to afford him any opportunity that life has to offer."

"For now he only wishes for a dog."

Darcy smiled. "He told me all about the Duke today and the man's dog. I should like to meet this kindly gentleman someday. When do you expect to see him next?"

Priscilla dropped a dish. "I—his appearances at the park are haphazard—I would not venture to guess."

"Can we at least afford more than the occasional maid?" Mrs. Sherwood bemoaned.

"Perhaps. Let us discuss the matter tomorrow. I had best be on my way."

She kissed her sister and stepmother. The activities at the gaming hall might distract her mind from continually wandering back to Radcliff and how she might never again feel his touch. Her body ached in response, punishing her for depriving it of the greatest pleasure it had ever known.

Despite her hope, the hours at Mrs. T's wore on without providing much comfort, the cards in front of her barely better than a blur. She kept expecting to see Radcliff walking in.

"Damn good beef-steak tonight," Henry said as he licked the juice off his fork.

The clock in the dining hall chimed eleven times.

"You've not touched yours," Henry noted of the plate before Darcy. "Never thought to see you rebuff a delectable cut of beef."

"I've not had much of an appetite these past few days," Darcy said.

"A sure symptom of being in love," Henry remarked softly.

"I would sooner have fallen in love with you, Harry, for all the good it does me."

"Lose the bosom and grow a—ahem—and I would be at your feet in seconds."

Darcy laughed. "I *do* love you, Harry."

"And I you, my dear. You've no notion how many times I wish you were a man."

"Life would be much simpler were that the case."

"Only I would still be insanely jealous of all the men that went your way. Now eat your steak like a good boy."

Darcy glanced at the meat and felt a pitching sensation in her stomach. She brought a hand to her mouth.

"I think not."

Henry frowned, then reached for her plate and set it down in his own place. "Can't let it go to waste."

"I miss him, Harry."

"I know it," Henry answered with a mouthful of steak. "You have been melancholy and pale. You move about rather listlessly, you refrain from eating."

"I had breakfast," Darcy pointed out.

"Aye, and nearly heaved it back onto my shoes."

"Yes, Priscilla did that once to me when she was a few months with Nathan…"

Henry stopped cutting into his steak and looked up abruptly at her. Darcy stared back with the widened eyes of a doe not knowing which way to turn.

"Dear God…" Henry breathed.

Darcy shook her head as if that alone could ward off the reality. But it permeated her nonetheless. The symptoms were too similar to what Priscilla had experienced. She was with child.

CHAPTER FOURTEEN

✺

IT WAS PAST TWO O'CLOCK in the morning and all but a handful of men remained in the card room at Mrs. T's. Not surprisingly, the remaining patrons sat at a table around Darcy. She laughed at their yarns and batted her lashes at their compliments. It was difficult to tell if she had partaken of a little too much wine.

One man brazenly circled his hand about her neck and pulled her mouth to his. Instead of recoiling, she returned his kiss. As she did so, another reached over and fondled her breast. She did not recoil from him either.

This was too much for the other three men. They each wanted a part of her. Soon all five sets of hands were upon her, groping her through her thin dress. She broke off her kiss with the first patron but her mouth quickly found another. They ripped the dress and undergarments from her until her breasts, belly, and legs were laid bare.

To better access her body, they lifted her onto the card table. Ten separate hands kneaded her breasts, pinched her nipples, caressed her thighs, squeezed her buttocks, and separated her legs. Darcy thrust herself into their ravenous grasps. She moaned in delight as one pair of hands separated her legs and reached towards her mons. A finger disappeared into her. She shuddered and begged for more. A second finger was shoved into her. A third. A fourth.

Two men attached their mouths to each of her nipples while their hands dove into their own pants. The fourth man climbed on top of the table, straddling her, pushed her breasts around his shaft and began thrusting himself between the two orbs. The man who had been fingering her *removed his hand and replaced it with his shaft. They each began to spend, hollering their climaxes. She bucked against the table with her own. She screamed for more...*

Radcliff woke from the dream to find his sheets damp with sweat and his erection painfully stiff. He grabbed himself and brought himself to spend. But while it relieved the pressure, it failed to wash away the feelings of emptiness, pain, anger and jealousy—remnants of both the dream as well as her visit.

How could she have refused him? He had mulled that question over a hundred times. At times, he wondered if he had done something wrong. At times, he blamed her for being what his aunt had considered her all along. A leopard does not change its spots, Anne might say. At least Darcy did not ask for nearly what she had demanded the first time they had met. He would have given her more than she asked.

Though that was little consolation. Radcliff would have almost preferred *not* to have the deed to Brayten in his hands. What should have been a moment of triumph was the most bitter experience of his life. It took all his strength to hand over those promissory notes. He wanted to strangle her. He wanted to kiss her with maddening desperation. He wanted to hold her and never let go.

But she would not have him. She had made that clear. He had been a dalliance. One mere chapter in her catalog of lovers.

The thought put him in a cross mood all day. He penned a message for Edward to see him and noticed that the servant was halfway out the door before the note even exchanged hands. As he waited for Edward to arrive, he attempted to read the newspaper, listened to his secretary give an account of the anticipated activities for the House of Lords, and met with his accountant regarding the trust for Edward.

But mostly he thought about Darcy. The prospect of being his mistress could not possibly be entirely disagreeable for her. He knew she was not immune to his touch. In fact, he believed she desired him as much as he did her. There had to be a way to convince her to be his.

Not being able to claim her, he felt an even greater desire to have her. He was in a constant state of agitation and nearly took the head off the servant knocking at his door.

"What is it?" he growled.

The servant he had sent to retrieve Edward timidly opened the door.

"Where have you been?" Radcliff demanded as he adjusted his pants beneath his writing desk. "One could have made it halfway to Gretna Green in the amount of time you have taken."

"Y-yes, your lordship. You told me not to return without Mr. Edward Barrington."

"And where is he?"

The servant began to quake in his boots. "Th-that be it, your lordship. I w-waited for him at his house. When he did—did not return for some time, I made some inquiries but—but to no avail. One of his servants thought, p-perhaps he had gone to Mrs. T.'s."

"What?" Radcliff thundered as he rose to his feet. "I gave him specific instructions…"

He saw the servant cower closer to the door as if ready to make a hasty escape.

"Have my horse ready and tell my valet to fetch my hat and gloves," Radcliff ordered.

The servant was only too happy to be out of Radcliff's presence. He scurried away like a mouse fearful that it was to be trampled upon by a galloping bull.

In his haste, Radcliff nearly knocked over one of his maidservants who had come to inform him that supper was ready.

"Give it to the parish orphans," he said. His cook always prepared too much damn food.

With his horse saddled and his valet greeting him at the door with his accoutrements, Radcliff was ready to make his way to Mrs. T. His hands itched to grab Edward by the collar. It was all Edward's fault. He would probably have never crossed paths with Darcy Sherwood if not for his cousin's folly.

The scene at the gaming hall was already boisterous when Radcliff arrived. He entered the card room, and though he had come for Edward, his eyes sought for her.

She sat at a round table surrounded by her usual admirers. Though a smile always played about her lips, her gaze seemed distant, much in the same way he had noticed the first day he saw her here. Again the longing to sweep her away swelled in his bosom.

She looked up and saw him, and her features tensed. Turning to the gentleman next to her, she began a heavy flirtation with him. Radcliff clenched his fists, and decided to look for Edward. If he watched for too much longer, he was likely to toss the man next to her from his seat or commit himself to a reckless duel.

But Edward was not to be found. One man he asked said that he had seen Edward but a few minutes before. Radcliff decided to sit down at a card table and wait for Edward to return, though in part he wanted to keep an eye on Darcy as well.

She had evidently not waited long before moving on to her next conquest. Would the bastard next to her receive a note inviting him to her bedchamber after all the festivities had waned? Would she tie him up as she had with him? Would she play with him, torment him or submit to the man's sexual desires?

He was making himself crazy, Radcliff realized as he looked down at his losing cards. He tossed the irritating cards back at the dealer. Where the goddamn hell was Edward?

"Perhaps your fortunes will change at the next hand," said a lilting voice.

Radcliff looked up to see the golden haired woman whom he had offended the first day he came to Mrs. T's. She sat down next to him and flashed him a smile. Apparently she did not recognize him or she had decided to overlook his initial rudeness.

"I can improve a man's fortunes," she purred, "sometimes in more ways than one."

"I am not here to seek fortunes," Radcliff responded as he glanced towards Darcy's table. "I am merely waiting for someone."

The woman followed his gaze. "You mean Sir William—the gentleman seated next to Miss Sherwood? Is he a friend of yours? I hear he has no need to seek fortunes either. Earned his fortune building ships for the war, I am told?"

Radcliff ground his teeth. It should not surprise him that Darcy would seek out a rich bastard.

"Did you come over from Belgium with him? All friends of Sir William are welcome here."

The blond had placed on his thigh under the card table. Radcliff turned his attention to her.

"Are you not a bit young to be bandying about a gaming hell?" he asked. "Shouldn't you be back in the schoolroom?"

"Do you prefer your women older?" she inquired with a tilt of her head. Her hand moved closer to his crotch. "I assure you younger women are more spirited. It more than compensates for experience."

"I can assure you it does not," Radcliff replied. "Where is your family?"

She frowned. "They live in Cornwall."

"Your mother and father are alive then? Have you brothers and sisters?"

"What silly questions you ask, sir," she laughed nervously.

"Have you?"

She pouted and answered with exasperation. "I have six sisters and two brothers—both younger, if you must know."

From the corner of his eye, Radcliff saw Darcy leave the table and exit the card room.

"Here's a hundred guineas. Go back to your family," Radcliff advised gently before rising from his own table.

The young woman stared at the money in her hands.

"There is no need to waste time, girl," he said. She looked at him with a mixture of gratitude and confusion but did as she was bid. After seeing her out of the card room, Radcliff hurried back to the hall where he had seen Darcy head. He saw her enter the drawing room with Edward.

He paused, wondering if he should storm into the room and demand what was afoot. Or should he merely press his ear to the door? Before he made a decision, Edward emerged from the room, cursing under his breath. A hand was pressed to his nose as if a foul stench was wafting all around him.

Instead of following his cousin, Radcliff turned toward the drawing room. He had barely crossed the threshold before he collided into Miss Sherwood.

"Kindly step from my path," she demanded after he had steadied from stumbling back.

"Not till you tell me what you and Edward were about in here," he said, his hands still upon her arms. God, how he wanted to crush her to him and take possession of her mouth with his.

Her eyes narrowed. "I wish to never lay eyes upon another Barrington as long as I live!"

She attempted to walk past him, but he held onto her. She seemed particularly angry and a little flustered. "What did you want with Edward?"

"What did *I* want? I would sooner he rot in hell, to be honest. It was *he* who wished to see me."

"And what did *he* want?" Radcliff demanded.

"To play one last hand for the deed to Brayten. I told him I had already returned it to you."

"And?"

She looked down at his grip upon her. "Unhand me. The touch of one Barrington is enough."

Radcliff felt his stomach drop. His anger turned to concern. "Did he dare lay a hand upon you? I swear to God I will box his ears in."

A small smile came to her lips. "Well, his ears may be one thing. His nose has already suffered and will not likely breathe easily for a while…my father taught me a few things about pugilism in addition to cards."

Relief washed over Radcliff. "Nonetheless, I'll whip the boy within inch of his life when I see him."

Her eyes narrowed once more. "Yes, when you see him, perhaps you should not encourage him."

"What do you mean?"

She pushed his hands away. "I am flattered that you think me a better frigging than a whore—"

"I would never confide such a thing to Edward."

She seemed to believe him, but her tone was still cold as she spoke. "Should you not return to Miss Dove? No doubt she is still waiting for you."

"Miss Who? Oh, the country girl. I sent her back to her family." Radcliff stiffened and eyed Darcy warily. "And you? You wish to return to Sir William I take it?"

"I did promise him another hand of piquet."

Radcliff grabbed her again. He felt as if he was going to go mad with jealousy.

"What else do you intend on promising him?"

"It is none of your affair if I wish to promise him anything!"

"At least he is an improvement over James Newcastle," Radcliff sneered. "Where is Newcastle today? Was his wealth not enough for you?"

She pressed her lips in a firm line of displeasure—lips he desperately wanted to kiss. "Pray find another gaming hall to hound and unhand me. I am not a possession of yours."

"But you are. Mine and mine alone."

"The arrogance of a Barrington is almost laughable."

He swung her around and pinned her to the wall. "Do you deny the desires of your own body? It craves the mastery of my touch."

He glanced down her décolletage at the swell of her breasts to her hips. His hands itched to lift the hem of her skirts. Lifting his gaze to her eyes, he saw a flicker of doubt. He would show her that she was his, that she needed to be his and longed to be his.

"Part your lips for me," he said, barely able to get the words out as he breathed in her scent. He stepped closer to her until he could feel the tips of her breasts against his chest.

"You forget that I am no longer in debt to you," she protested a little too desperately.

"It matters not," he responded. "You will do as I bid."

He ran his thumb along her nipple and felt her body shudder.

"Not anymore, my lord."

Radcliff smiled to himself. *My lord*. The words had come out naturally of their own accord. He drew his body up against hers so that she could feel his hardened arousal against her belly. He heard her inhale sharply. The heat of their breath warmed the room. If he did not take her soon, his body would surely overheat and melt the clothes he was wearing.

"I have patrons to attend to," she said.

"They can wait."

With an aggravated cry, she pushed him away.

"Fifty shillings," she choked. "The price to lay me will cost you fifty shillings."

He stared blankly at her.

"Fifty shillings," she repeated, trembling.

Radcliff could hardly believe his ears. He searched her eyes, which shone bright with emotion, but could not detect any indication that she spoke in jest.

"Darcy," he pleaded.

"Miss Sherwood, if you please."

This was not how he had imagined it could be between them.

"If the price be too rich for your blood, I suggest you step aside that I may find a man who will pay it," she said before brushing by him without another word.

☾

THE WEATHER PERFORMED PERFECTLY FOR the Pinkerton garden party. A slight breeze, only enough to ruffle the feathers and ribbons of a lady's hat, tempered the warmth of the sun's rays. Lord Pinkerton's many flora were reaching the end of their blooms, and he was more than happy to provide them one last show.

On the receiving end of Lord Pinkerton's explanation of which flowers were more difficult to cultivate and which he expected to import next year, Radcliff listened with an occasional nod but allowed his friend the majority of the conversation.

"Ah, and this one," Lord Pinkerton said lovingly of a blue flower as if it were his daughter, "this one did not seem to take to our

English soil at first, but it had an inner strength, and as you can see, has flourished, outlasting the annuals that used to grow here."

After a pause in which he smiled with admiration down at the flower, Pinkerton continued, "Rather reminds me of that raven beauty who came to my ball—the uninvited guest of Lady Worthley. Miss Sherwood. How does she fare?"

Inwardly, Radcliff cringed, a hollow feeling reverberating throughout his body. "I know not. I haven't seen her in over three fortnights."

He had been tempted numerous times to seek her out despite her coldness to him. Despite her words that suggested he was of no more consequence than any of her other lovers—or less than a lover for it cost him fifty bloody shillings. And while he was not one to give up easily, he was not a fool to be where he was clearly not wanted.

She clearly did not feel the same way he did. He desired Darcy Sherwood more than anything he had ever desired in his life. Desired not only her body. But the thrill he derived from bringing her pleasure. The sense of achievement when he brought a smile to her lips. He missed their easy conversations. The peace he felt when he held her in his arms. He desired even the anger that his arrogance provoked in her.

"No need to, I suppose, now that the deed to Brayten is returned to Edward?" Pinkerton inquired.

"Brayten will be held in a trust for an indeterminate time," Radcliff answered. He did not need to explain to Pinkerton, who nodded with comprehension, the reason. Nor did he disclose how he had nearly refused to return Brayten to Edward at all.

After his last visit to Darcy, he had found Edward back at home nursing his battered nose.

"Bitch damn near broke my nose," Edward had exclaimed after Radcliff had confronted him about being at Mrs. T's.

To which Radcliff had decided to complete the task by leveling his right hook square in the center of Edward's face. He had then grabbed Edward by the collar in one hand, lifting him to his feet, and thrown him against the wall.

"And if you ever dare lay a hand upon Miss Sherwood," Radcliff had said, "by God, if you so much as glance in her direction, I will break every bone in your body."

He had not realized how strongly he had been gripping Edward's throat until the latter started turning blue in the face. With disgust, he had released his hold of Edward, who had fallen to the floor on his knees, gasping and wheezing.

Radcliff decided the boy was lucky to have escaped his wrath with only a broken nose.

"Should you, er, decide to pursue the company of Miss Sherwood," Pinkerton said, breaking into Radcliff's thoughts about how easily and willingly he would have broken the noses of a fleet of men who dared to touch Darcy, "know that I will be there to back you."

Radcliff raised his brows.

"You would lose your entrée into Almack's, of course," Pinkerton continued. "I fear women can be rather harsh, but you have far too much standing and respect from most of your peers to be cast out entirely."

"Your words of support are much appreciated," Radcliff responded with tenderness for his old friend, "but she will have none of me."

It was Pinkerton's turn to raise his brows. "Indeed?"

"I believe she is content in her situation at the Tillinghast gaming hall."

"How can that be?"

Radcliff shrugged. Not particularly interested in pursuing the current course of conversation, he said simply. "She is the daughter of Jonathan Sherwood."

"That she is," Pinkerton conceded and, to Radcliff's relief, decided to resume his discourse on the best climate and water conditions for day lilies.

"Thank God the whole horrid affair is at an end," Anne Barrington said a few moments later to Radcliff when tea was being served.

Radcliff had hoped to leave the party without exchanging a

word with Anne, but Juliana had begged him to stay. The three of them sat at one of the small tables that had been laid out in the garden for tea.

"But don't you think you were rather harsh on Edward—on us?" Anne admonished. "I understand placing Brayten in a trust, but the allowance you have allocated for him can hardly sustain the most frugal miser. After all, the poor boy has suffered so much at the hand of that harlot. Did you hear that she attempted to break his nose?"

Staring hard at his aunt, Radcliff wondered if certain mothers would forever overlook the trespasses of their offspring.

"She failed miserably," Radcliff returned icily, "so I took the liberty of breaking it myself."

Anne choked on the biscuit and looked at her nephew as if he were mad.

"And I would not hesitate to break it again if he ever speaks ill of Miss Sherwood," he added and fixed upon his aunt such an ominous stare that one would think he was threatening to break *her* nose.

"As for the matter of his allowance," Radcliff continued, "the majority of what would have been his will be used to support your grandson."

"My *what?*"

"A responsibility he has grossly neglected. He is fortunate that the Sherwoods want nothing to do with him—a fortune he little deserves."

"I suggest," he said as he stood up. He could not bear his aunt's company any longer, not even for Juliana, "that you thank the Sherwoods in your prayers each evening."

With his aunt stunned wordless, he executed a curt bow to Juliana and headed back inside the house.

"My hat and gloves," he told one of the servants.

He would have return to his county seat, Radcliff decided. He was weary of London and the *ton* with all her meddlers and gossipers. Most of all, he needed a respite of anything that reminded him of Darcy Sherwood.

"Cousin!"

Radcliff turned to find Juliana bounding down the hall towards him.

"How old is he?" Juliana asked. "What is his name?"

"He is being taken care of," Radcliff answered. "You need not trouble yourself."

"But he is my nephew, is he not?" Juliana pursed her lips together. "I had a suspicion that Edward and Miss Priscilla—though I was quite young back then. Such matters were mainly beyond my comprehension."

How Juliana managed to become half intelligent and not made into an addlepated young woman by her mother was a marvel to Radcliff. There was hope for her yet, he decided.

"Will you be seeing the Sherwoods soon?" Juliana inquired.

"No," Radcliff said flatly.

Juliana frowned. "Oh. I had hoped to meet Miss Sherwood again."

"I suggest you return to tend to your mother. She has been dealt a shock—"

"When do you expect to see Miss Sherwood next?"

"I do not expect to see Miss Sherwood again," he responded as he accepted the hat and gloves that a servant had brought.

"But why?"

"She would rather I not."

"But how is that possible? Did you upset her?"

Radcliff glanced sharply at his cousin, reconsidering his earlier praise of Juliana. He responded with some irritation, "If I did, it is no affair of yours."

"I beg your pardon, cousin. Only it seemed you were quite taken with her," Juliana persisted with a naivete that made it hard for anyone to become too angry with her.

"I was—but she refused me." He hoped that would put an end to Juliana's line of questioning and turned to leave.

Juliana's eyes widened. "Refused you? It is unbelievable that anyone would refuse to marry *you*."

"I did not offer..." Radcliff stopped. It was inappropriate to be talking of mistresses before his young cousin.

"But especially Miss Sherwood," Juliana went on. "She adored you."

Radcliff turned around again. "What do you mean?"

And how the devil would you know? he wanted to say to the little chit.

"I saw it at the ball. In her eyes when she looked your way. And she did look your way quite a number of times, though she pretended not to. It seemed quite apparent that you were the reason she came to the ball."

Was that what Pinkerton had been trying to allude to as well? Radcliff wondered. His demeanor softened towards his cousin.

"Be that as it may," he said, "Miss Sherwood has made it clear that henceforth, she has no interest in pursuing our acquaintance."

"Forgive me, cousin, if what I am to say next should be considered brazen, but I did not think you were one to...to quit easily."

"It was indeed brazen," Radcliff told her, then felt a stab of guilt when she hung her head, but he had no need for his niece to question his manhood. "I appreciate your concern, but you need not trouble yourself of my affairs."

Juliana opened her mouth, but this time Radcliff would not allow her to delay his departure further. He bid her adieu and proceeded home.

☾

"A HUNDRED SHILLINGS," DARCY TOLD HENRY as they sat in the dining room again the following evening—at the very same table she used to sit at with Radcliff.

"Don't seem right," Henry grumbled. "What sort of medical background has this man? I hear most of his kind are little more than witch doctors."

"I haven't much of a choice," Darcy replied. "I do *not* want another Barrington bastard."

But even as she spoke these words, she felt a sense of loss, torn between wanting to keep the last evidence of Radcliff and not wanting to be reminded of the man who broke her heart.

"Very well," Henry relented. "I'll secure you a hundred shillings."

Darcy shook her head. "You've not a hundred shillings to spare, Harry. I see your new lover has a new suit of clothes. He is not a man of means and is terrible at cards."

Henry flushed and looked down at his plate of half-eaten food.

"And I require more than a hundred shillings," Darcy added.

"What of the money from Broadmoor?"

"The first installment won't be enough to discharge all the bills and pay for Nathan's tutor."

"Have you appealed to Mathilda?"

"She can loan me two hundred, far short of what I need."

Henry knit his brows. "There must be some way…would you consider Newcastle?"

The name made her shudder. "He has not been as attentive to me as of late and—"

"That can easily change. You have only to sneeze in his direction."

"And I could not bring myself to ask him," Darcy finished. "I could not be beholden to that man. It takes all my strength not to recoil from his touch."

A woman at the other end of the dining hall squealed. Darcy turned to see Cavin Richards at a table with a brunette. He was leaning into the table at an awkward angle, and Darcy had a suspicion, though the tablecloth hid it, that he had his hand upon the woman's leg—or further.

The thought entered both her and Henry at the same time.

"Do you suppose he would…" Henry asked.

"Worth asking, I suppose," Darcy answered.

She turned the idea about in her head throughout the evening. Her luck at the table was middling, and she could not help but think it fortuitous that Cavin should be here the night she might need him. Smartly dressed in a burgundy coat and beige trousers, he was a much admired Corinthian. He certainly had the fiduciary means to assist her.

How she dreaded asking others for help. Her father had never done it well, to his family's detriment. And it was only thoughts of Priscilla and Nathan that gave her enough courage to swallow her pride. Nathan would have the respect he deserved. She would not allow the Barringtons to defeat her family.

"Mr. Richards," she approached after she had battled down her hesitation. "I desire a word with you, if you will."

"There is no 'if' where Miss Sherwood is concerned," Cavin replied. "Summon and I come."

He excused himself from his companion for the evening and followed Darcy into the small library used only by those seeking a quick and quiet tryst.

"I have need of a loan, Cavin," she blurted with the door barely closed. "Of about a thousand pounds."

Cavin looked bemused. After a moment's pause as he realized she was in earnest, he responded, "Well, you don't tarry about the bush, do you? That's a grand sum of money. If it is funds you seek to borrow, why not apply to old Wempole? I am no banker."

"Wempole is no longer in a position to lend me what I require."

"And what of Broadmoor?"

Darcy felt her cheeks flame. "I doubt he will be seen here anymore."

His brows shot up, but he did not inquire further. It was a virtue Darcy appreciated in him—Cavin never pressed for more information and perhaps because he did not care.

"I shall pay it back with interest," Darcy added as she watched him approach her.

"How delightful," he murmured, reaching out to curl a tendril of her hair about his finger.

"Not *that* sort of interest, Richards."

"But the interest is what interests me, eh?"

"I am in earnest."

"Tell you what," Cavin drawled as he relinquished her hair. "This be a gaming hall, I shall play you for it. High card draw. If you win, the money is yours. If I win, your price will be your body for the night—given to me as once you used to."

Her breath caught in her throat. It had been years since they had shared a bed, but even then their company had been simply a joining of flesh, of two people who enjoyed the carnal pleasures. As Darcy studied the twinkle in his grey eyes and how his hair falling over his eyes only seemed to improve his rakish appeal, she began to wonder if perhaps a tumble with someone like Cavin wasn't exactly what she needed to drive out all thoughts of Radcliff.

Her lips curled in a half smile at his resourcefulness, and she replied, "You flatter me."

Cavin bowed. "Indeed, I have never offered a woman anywhere near a thousand pounds for the privilege of bedding her. However, no other woman comes close to being Miss Darcy Sherwood."

"A fact that has not stopped you."

"As with you, Miss Sherwood, I am more gourmet than gourmand. Variety is the spice of life."

Darcy did not dispute him, though she knew his comparison no longer to hold truth. She had fallen in love with Radcliff Barrington and wanted no other man.

But it was not to be and she needed the money.

"Very well," Darcy assented. She walked over to a writing desk, pulled out a pack of cards, shuffled the desk, and presented it to Cavin.

CHAPTER FIFTEEN

"LADIES FIRST," CAVIN INSISTED.

Taking a deep breath, she pulled up a ten of spades and felt a small sense of relief. There was less than a third of a chance that he could win.

Cavin smiled and casually held up a jack of diamonds.

"Well, don't look thrilled," he said upon seeing her frown.

"I don't suppose you would lend me the thousand when our night is over?" Darcy tried.

"Perhaps I would entertain a wager double or nothing."

Darcy did not respond. She had to wait and see how she would feel after the first night.

"I shall have to bid adieu to the lady at my table," Cavin informed her as he headed towards the doors. "But I shall be in your chambers shortly. No need to send the page—I remember the way."

He winked at her before departing. Darcy sank onto the settee. *Damn.* Now not only would she have to service Cavin, she had not a crown more than she had started the night with. It wasn't that she didn't find Cavin attractive. In fact, once they had concluded their affair, she had avoided any further physical contact for fear that they would end up once again in that uncertain territory of unspoken attachments that easily led to jealousy and pain. She had certainly been tempted through the years.

Until Radcliff had entered her world. And now she found it hard to contemplate being with anyone else.

She rose and went to pour herself a glass of wine at the sideboard. Well, perhaps she should make use of this occasion. Being with Cavin would remind her of the days when coupling was but a corporal release, to serve an animal instinct. To harbor delusions that she could have anything more than that with a man would only set herself up for certain disappointment, as her experience with Broadmoor had proved.

Darcy poured a second glass after finishing the first. Radcliff Barrington had served his purpose. She had her prior debt taken care of and an income that would total fifty-five thousand pounds—more than she had ever thought possible prior to winning the deed to Brayten. What more did she truly expect? That he had taken her senses to new heights was an unexpected perquisite to the bargain.

The memory of their stolen moment in the garden warmed her as much as the wine. She settled into the settee with her third glass, and her hand crept down to lift the hem of her dress. When he touched her, it seemed she could think of nothing else but spending for him. Nothing else existed but the two of them and the need for their bodies to join together. She remembered being sandwiched between his hard body and the equally hard tree. She closed her eyes and clenched her thighs. How she wanted to take him in so many ways. She had not come close to exhausting her repertoire of seducing a man and making him spend. She had enjoyed succumbing to his commands, but she had also looked forward to righting the ship and issuing a few of her own.

She gulped the rest of her wine. She had to stop tormenting herself with such thoughts. Rising to her feet, she went to pour herself another glass. Gazing into the liquid, she wished that she could drink the Baron Broadmoor into a distant memory. The cards would not do it. She was sure to look for him after every hand.

The wine splashed down her throat. She barely tasted it. There were other men. More than enough vying for her attention. Perhaps they would make her forget him. And she could start with Cavin. Yes, Cavin. Devilishly handsome Cavin. Devilish Cavin.

He was just the man she needed. He would remind her of the person she ought to return to being. Not this pained, lovesick woman.

She poured herself a third glass for a part of her deep within doubted that he would prove as much the antidote as she had hoped. Finishing her wine, she readied herself for Cavin.

The hallway was starting to sway before her eyes as she made her way up the staircase. Perhaps she should not have had that final glass, but it felt pleasant.

"Beggin' pardon," Cavin said behind her, "I could not extricate myself from the company as easily as I thought."

"Meaning you wanted to play another round of hazard," Darcy clarified for him.

Cavin grinned as he swept her hand to his lips. "I am all yours, *ma cheri*. You look every bit as enchanting as the day I met you."

"I drew the lower card—you've no need to flatter me."

"I know," he said in a husky voice and stared into her eyes in manner that would have made any other woman swoon. He reached out a hand to cup her cheek before bringing her head to his. His lips brushed hers lightly, teasing her of what was to come. It differed from the deep and probing kisses from Radcliff. With Cavin, lovemaking was like the art of fencing. He advanced, then retreated, then advanced again to keep the other forever guessing.

Now his kiss deepened, forcing her lips apart for his tongue. They stumbled against the door of her bedroom. Darcy allowed him to guide the dance for she was unsure if she could coordinate her body if she tried. He opened the door without removing his mouth from hers and backed her into the room. A lamp was already lit—an odd occurrence—but this was to be no ordinary night.

After tossing his hat aside and peeling off his coat, he pulled up the hem of her dress and petticoat and lifted her by the thighs. She wrapped her legs around his waist. Now she remembered. But what she wanted was to be done with it all. She fumbled to untie his cravat while he carried her towards the bed. Perhaps, if she employed her skills well, she would have him spending shortly. And Cavin always fell asleep afterwards.

"God, it has been too long," he mumbled as he kissed her neck and his favorite spot behind the ear.

Despite herself, Darcy arched her back. Perhaps she should enjoy the moment, the wine suggested. She stared up at the ceiling as he trailed his mouth down to bite a nipple through her bodice. The room gently rocked before her as she struggled with what to do.

Lose yourself in Cavin and forget about Radcliff, one voice offered.

Absent-mindedly, she reached down and stroked his erection through his trousers. It seemed her mind could not complete a thought. She could not remember when wine had had such a strong effect on her.

Cavin groaned, and Darcy recognized he was about to reach the point when the fencing would be over and he wanted only one thing. She watched as he hastily took off his waistcoat and shed his boots and trousers. Cavin rarely ever bothered to undress his women, unlike Radcliff, who seemed to enjoy viewing her naked body much like one appreciating a fine painting.

She remembered the way his eyes would light up upon seeing her. She imagined the tongue caressing her was that of Radcliff. Her body responded to the idea, and her wetness grew. What would Radcliff do next? Would he cup her buttocks as he tongued her? Reach up and caress her breasts? Would he turn her around and spank her for rebuffing him?

A moan escaped her. A reflection of what her body longed for, though no doubt Cavin would interpret that as him. He climbed into bed and pulled her on top of him. This was his favorite position, she recalled. The effects of the wine were at their strongest, and her body felt warm, in need of contact.

"You and I belong together, *ma cheri*," Cavin said as she settled on his hips and wrapped her hand about his hard cock. "Broadmoor could not appreciate you as I can."

But he did, a voice inside her protested.

"Only a fool would fail to appreciate the essence of Miss Sherwood."

Her heart hammered against her ribs. Had she heard correctly?

She was afraid to turn around to find out.

"By Jove, have you been here the whole of the time?" she heard Cavin say.

And then she knew, without looking, where he was: sitting in the same chair he had occupied that first night he had surprised her in her bedroom. She felt like crumbling into little pieces. This would only confirm his opinion of her as a wanton harlot. She turned her head to the side and saw him from the corner of her eye. He was looking at Cavin, his knuckles white.

"Damn near scared me half to bloody death," Cavin continued.

"That would not be my intention," Radcliff replied in a tone that suggested he considered such an unintended prospect a happy consequence nonetheless. He turned to leave.

Darcy felt her internal organs cringe. She was tempted to speak, but what could she say? Cavin, however, had no problem with words.

"Care to join us?" he asked.

Darcy felt her eyes bulge from their sockets. She could sense Radcliff's body tensing and hoped that he could contain his desire to strangle Cavin.

"Merely jesting, ole chap," Cavin said, swinging his legs off the bed. "I take it you came to have a word with Miss Sherwood *in private.*"

"What I had to say is unimportant," Radcliff returned as he turned to leave without the barest glance in her direction.

It was just as well for she wanted nothing more than to disappear into the earth.

"Hold yourself," Cavin insisted, glancing between the two of them. He stood on his feet. "I know you don't think me much of a gentleman, Broadmoor, but I know my priority with Miss Sherwood. Worry not, you've not interrupted anything—yet."

Collecting his coat, he turned to her and raised her hand to his lips. "Adieu, *ma cheri*. Let us say you owe me a song and call our wager even."

Darcy blinked her eyes. Dear Cavin! She had not thought such selflessness in him. Gratefully, she watched him depart.

Now she had to face Radcliff alone, and the look on his face was far more daunting than she had ever seen.

But he made it somewhat easier for her when he said, "I see you did not wait long to return to your old ways."

She swung her legs off the bed and caught him staring at her bare ankle before her gown fell back into place. The wine in her gave her courage. "La, sir, what did you expect from a harlot?"

If she could make it to the door…but the threshold seemed twice as far in her current state of inebriation. And the damn thing kept moving its position.

She stumbled. He caught her. She jerked herself from his hold.

"Unhand me," she hissed. "Lest you wish to pay for the privilege of your touch."

A muscle rippled along his jaw. Without word, he swept her into his arms and strode to her bed. He dropped her unceremoniously onto it.

"And what did Richards pay?" he growled, pinning her body beneath his.

She struggled beneath the weight of him but was hampered by both the wine and his strength.

"Nothing," she answered truthfully, convinced that that would send him away in a fury.

It did not, though fury flamed in his eyes. "You belong to me."

The bloody arrogance! She thrashed harder, but his mouth clamped down upon hers, forcing her lips open. He pressed down upon her hard. Her attempts to scream became muffled. And she was lost. Lost beneath the force of it. He delved deep as if he intended to leave his mark, as if he meant to claim her through the kiss. She felt her determination slipping and arousal taking its place. But as much as she wanted to, she would not kiss him back. She could not give him that satisfaction.

When at last he allowed her a breath, she spat, "I wouldn't lay you at any price."

"Indeed? You would forswear my touch—and how it makes you feel?"

She chanced to look into his eyes and became more desperate

to escape. But his mouth descended once more and pressed its heat to her throat.

"Forswear my kisses…" he said into her neck. His hand grasped a breast. "Forswear my caress…"

She could not hold back a moan. He lifted the hems of her dress and petticoats, but she did not try to stop him. Her body knew what it wanted: him. And when his fingers met her wetness, he would know it, too. As his digits strummed her arousal, his lips joined with hers. This time she returned the kiss, grinding her hips against his hand. The wine had dulled the sharpness of her senses even as it fueled her desire. It was not long before he had her body jolting and shuddering against him.

Quickly he shed his coat and unbuttoned his pants. His arousal was hard as flint. He did not enter her gently or gradually. He speared his shaft into her and buried himself to the hilt. She gasped, but the power of his desire, the depth of his jealousy excited her. At least he lusted for her, even if he could not love her enough to marry her. She bucked against him with as much vigor as she could muster in a show of anger to match his.

The bed rattled and struck the wall. Her cries and his grunts filled the room. Her breasts swung uncomfortably beneath him. He pushed her legs up to her chest to penetrate even deeper. She dug her fingers into his flesh and braced herself for the violent orgasm that blasted through her with the force of a cannon. Groaning low, he thrust fast and furious and roared with his own release. He fell on top of her, his breath coming hard, his hair dampened with sweat.

As her body reassembled itself from its shattered state, through the haze, she exalted in the feel of his weight atop her.

She would blame the wine, she decided. Surely he could see that she was foxed. If she had her wits about herself, she would not have let this happen. Even though it had felt beyond wonderful.

C

HIS FURY GONE, ONLY TENDERNESS filled its place as Radcliff collected her in his arms. He kissed the perspiration on her nose, swept his lips across her closed eyes. Surely she understood how she belonged to him. That they belonged to each other.

He kissed her through her hair. "Be mine, Darcy."

She opened her eyes and turned to him. "Your what? Your mistress? Your whore?"

Her tone made him wince.

"I spoke of it before," she said. "I am no man's mistress."

"Because you've a wish to return to Richards?"

It was not what he had meant to say, but he could not help the anger that leaped into his throat.

She scrambled out of bed and began desperately looking for something. Pulling out a chamber pot, she heaved into it.

"I have matters to attend," she said, hastily donning a shift and throwing her dress on top sans a corset.

He watched her leave and cursed himself for a fool. He had allowed the sentimental words of Juliana and Pinkerton to cloud his rationale. And so he had sought out Miss Sherwood to make one final overture, only to find her lifting her skirts to Cavin Richards. He could easily have broken Richards' neck in twain in his jealousy. How he had managed to contain his fury surprised even him.

There was no returning here, he realized. A dagger through the heart would have been less painful than the prospect of never seeing her again, but he could not bear to watch her playing the coquette or taking another man to bed. Grabbing his coat, he strode out of her chamber. And out of her life.

"Leaving so soon?" a voice behind him asked as he walked past the card room downstairs.

It was the last voice Radcliff would have wanted to hear. He turned to face Richards, trying his best not to find some way to call Cavin out so that he might have the chance of running a blade through the man.

Cavin ignored the angry glare directed at him and took some snuff. "Reckon she may change her mind.".

Radcliff felt the hair on the back of his neck standing on end. He had no desire for a *tête-à-tête* with Cavin.

"About being your mistress," Cavin provided–

That Richards somehow knew the reason for his visit only incensed Radcliff more.

"She took you to bed willingly," continued Cavin.

Either the man was oblivious of the wrath he was incurring in Radcliff or was simply choosing to ignore it. Radcliff decided it was best to leave before he cuffed Richards on the jaw.

"I had to wager a hundred shillings for the privilege."

Remembering Darcy's words from before, Radcliff stopped and pulled out some money to toss onto a table.

"You can wager fifty shillings less next time," he said before walking out.

☙

"I LOST THE COURAGE TO DO it," Darcy explained to Henry as they sat in the box with Lady Worthley, who was accompanying an ailing friend who adored the opera. Lady Worthley was not nearly as enamored of operas and had asked Darcy and Henry for company.

"Then you mean to have the child?" Henry asked as he lifted the opera glasses to his eyes to scan the crowd for an interesting face—or body.

Darcy shook her head. "I could not. And yet I could not bring myself to ask for it. He said he would only require ten shillings for the visit."

"He's a bloody thief."

"It doesn't have to be a bastard," Henry piped up after they had walked in silence for a while. "I could marry you. Then you wouldn't have to put yourself at risk with that sham of a physician."

Darcy smiled and put a hand on her friend's arm. "Harry, a friend more true than you could not be had, but I would be of no use to Mrs. T as a married woman."

"No need to work at Mrs. T's once I am Earl of Brent. I will have an income of over ten thousand pounds per annum."

"But it may be years before you are Earl. Till then you have not enough to support two additional persons. And what will become of Priscilla and Nathan?"

"Perhaps my father would increase my allowance. Daresay he would be happy to have a marriage that would put an end to the rumors he pretends not to hear. You and I would make the perfect husband and wife, Darcy, as surely you would not mind my lovers and I would not mind yours. Or perhaps we could trade our lovers every now and then."

The gleam in his eyes brought both laughter and tears for Darcy.

"Your father would not approve of your marrying someone of my sort," she said. "The Earl of Brent, no matter what his proclivities, could ensnare a much better wife than I would be. But I do appreciate the thought, Harry. With all my heart I do."

They walked, her arm encircled about his, almost as if they were husband and wife.

"Perhaps I should have a word with Broadmoor," Henry thought aloud.

"Don't you dare," Darcy responded quickly. "He and I have done with one another."

Henry sighed for the both of them. He paused before saying, "You don't suppose I would have a chance with him?"

Darcy laughed again. "I don't think he was ever partial to you. I suspect he thought us lovers."

"Well then, I can prove that wrong!"

Darcy shook her head. "What an incorrigible man you are, Harry."

"And you love me for it." He lifted her hand to his lips.

"Be careful, Harry. I may fall in love with you and decide to marry you afterall."

Henry merely grinned. They wound their way around the

block back towards the gaming hall. A wistful comfort settled about Darcy. This was the life she knew. Henry, Mathilda, and the patrons of the gaming hall were the people she knew. For a brief moment her world had crossed with that of Radcliff Barrington, but like planets aligned before the sun, they would eventually part their separate ways.

And it was better that way.

❦

TRYING HIS BEST TO SUPPRESS a yawn, Radcliff shifted in his seat as the strains of *Orfeo and Euridice* filled the opera house. He was not as interested in early classical music and had not thought Juliana to be either, but he had agreed to escort his cousin to the performance nonetheless. He found shortly upon arriving that indeed it had not been the compositions of Christoph Willibald Gluck who held her interest but that of a young man sitting in the box next to them.

He seemed a decent fellow, though he did not possess as high a station in life as Radcliff would have liked for Juliana—Anne would disapprove without a second glance at the young man—but where one stood in the eyes of the *ton* mattered less to Radcliff. He allowed Juliana and the young man, Robert Gibbons, to have their moment during intermission. Radcliff stood far enough from the couple as not to intrude upon their conversation, feigning interest in what Mrs. Trindlewood and her daughter had to say.

Mrs. Trindlewood was quite amiable, but there was a nervousness about her. It seemed to Radcliff there was a hushed anxiety among many people he knew. He felt as if many glances were cast his way. He caught the eye of Juliana, and she seemed to look upon him with concern. He managed to extricate himself from Mrs. Trindlewood and approached Juliana and young Gibbons.

"Good day to you, sir," Robert greeted.

"Thank you, and a good evening to you," Radcliff responded.

Robert flushed as he realized he had referenced the wrong part of the day.

"Shall we to our seats?" Radcliff asked Juliana.

Her eyes were gleaming and he had never known her smile to be so wide. Then it had gone well despite the look of concern she had had earlier.

"Robert is a bit of a composer himself," Juliana told him. "He met Mozart."

"I was a mere boy," Robert said. "But his music did inspire me."

"I rather wish we were listening to one of his operas tonight instead."

Robert nodded. "Although, it can be said that Gluck paved the way for Mozart."

"Indeed. Perhaps you can tell me more of Mozart," Radcliff offered. "I am partial to Brooks's. Have you ever been?"

"No, sir."

"Then I should be happy to extend you an invitation as my guest."

Juliana made a sound somewhat like a puppy, and Robert pumped Radcliff by the hand numerously. When they had all returned to their boxes, Juliana grasped Radcliff by the arm.

"My dearest cousin!" she cried. "How can I ever thank you?"

"Delay your gratitude. I have not yet given him my blessing," Radcliff said. "I thought at one point you were not enjoying your *tête-à-tête*?"

"Oh, that." Juliana released him and looked away. "It was of no consequence."

He sensed an uneasiness from her, but put up his quizzing glass to take another look at Robert, who sat with his mother, father, and two brothers. His gaze wandered past their box, and he stiffened.

It couldn't be.

It was.

Darcy Sherwood. She was sitting with Wyndham, Lady Worthley, and an older woman he could not name.

Despite her worn and slightly dated gown, she looked beautiful.

Different. Fragile. Her hair had been set in curlers and arranged on top of her head and fixed with a jeweled hairpiece. But he was reminded of how much he liked her hair loose and even unruly. He was filled with a sense of loss that he would most likely never again see her hair tumbling in disarray about her. He wondered what brought her to the opera house.

"Cousin?"

Juliana's voice came to him as if from the end of a tunnel.

"I take it you have found Miss Sherwood."

Radcliff lowered his eye piece.

"That explains the look of concern I have been receiving all evening," he stated, "and what has set the tongues to twitter. One would think the gossips have tired of it all by now."

Juliana bit her lower lip. "That and…"

"And?" He fixed a daunting stare at her as he lifted his brows.

"It is said that she will wed the Viscount Wyndham."

Blood drained from him. To where, he knew not. When he recovered from the unexpected blow, he was besieged by a multitude of feelings. Anger. Jealousy. Pain. Loss. She was lost to him forever. His worst fear come to life. Only he had not put words to that fear for he had never conceived that she would marry, given that she had refused his offer.

Only his had not been one of matrimony.

The Viscount Wyndham. Well that was not quite the surprise given their obvious friendship. And the man would come into substantial wealth when he became the Earl of Brent. He had at times thought with confidence that Wyndham only cared for his own sex, but this proved otherwise. It was said that Wyndham had a lover.

This would not do. Nathan Barrington could not be brought up in a household filled with debauchery.

Radcliff signaled for the page. He scrawled a note and told the man to deliver it to the Viscount Wyndham.

CHAPTER SIXTEEN

❧

"**W**HAT DO YOU MEAN, PRISCILLA? How can that be?"
Darcy asked in disbelief despite the obvious agony in
her sister's eyes.

"I received this by courier today," Priscilla explained and handed
over a letter.

The seal, though broken, was clearly that of the Baron Barrington. Darcy took the letter and scanned its contents.

> *Dear Miss Priscilla Sherwood,*
> *It has come to my attention that young Nathan is not being
> afforded the advantages worthy of a Barrington. He is at a crit-
> ical age when great care must be attended to his upbringing. I
> mean to cast no aspersions on the care you have provided him
> thus far, but there are limits to what your family can offer him.
> As such, Nathan should be retained in my custody to ensure
> that he receives the full breadth of what is due to him.*
> *Your servant,*
> *R. Barrington*

It was brief and very much in the style of Radcliff. Even the
bold but elegant handwriting could not have been formed by any
hand other than his.

"Worthy of a Barrington?" Darcy recited from the letter, confused. "Does he believe Nathan to be Edward's then?"

Priscilla colored. "He is certain."

But surely he would have mentioned such knowledge, Darcy thought but then recalled Radcliff's growing interest in Nathan throughout their conversations. Then there was the suspicious matter of Nathan's new clothes and books...

"The tutor," Darcy said quickly, "the clothes...was Rad—was *he* providing those?"

Priscilla nodded with guilt.

"But how did he come to know? Did you speak to him?"

"He came upon us in the park," Priscilla explained. "Quite by accident—I think. Though it was rather strange that he should be at our park of all places. But when he saw Nathan—you know the resemblance Nathan bears to Edward—it became quite plain, I think."

"How is it you have not told me this?" Darcy cried as a dozen thoughts whirled and collided in her mind.

"He swore me to secrecy. For what reason, I know not, though I imagine it had something to do with his association with you..."

This time it was Darcy who colored.

"Have you fallen in love with him?"

Priscilla would have done better had she slapped Darcy across the face with all her might.

"You have, haven't you?" Priscilla persisted.

"It matters not," Darcy replied, then wished she had not spoken so sharply when she glanced a pained look in her sister's face. "Forgive me, Priscilla, I should have confided in you—as you should have confided in me. I told myself that I wished to protect you, Nathan, and mama from the scandal."

"We do not live on a separate continent, dear sister. We heard rumors almost from the beginning. But even were it not for the gossip, it was plain on your face how you felt—at least to me."

Darcy felt tears pressing against the back of her eyes as she received her sister's sympathetic smile.

"I suppose," Darcy said, "I was too mortified. Imagine two Sherwood sisters both falling for a Barrington!"

Darcy could see the tears in Priscilla's eyes as well. Without word, Priscilla threw her arms about Darcy.

They drew strength from each other, and when Priscilla pulled from the embrace, she said with half a laugh, "Those Barrington men are such horrid creatures, are they not?"

"Yes," Darcy answered but there was no jest in her voice as she recalled the letter she held. "'Worthy of a Barrington'...typical Barrington arrogance! For five years they did not lift a finger for Nathan—did not deign to acknowledge his existence—and now they wish to take him from us?"

"Had I known him better..." Priscilla began, "He seemed to have such a wonderful rapport with Nathan...and when Nathan so adored his dog..."

"The Duke that Nathan speaks of. It was Baron Broadmoor, then?"

"Yes, but, oh, I never conceived that he would try to take Nathan from me!"

"He most assuredly will *not* take Nathan from us," Darcy pronounced as she clenched the letter in her hand.

"But—"

"I will defend with my last breath our family. The Baron will rue the day he ever laid eyes upon a Sherwood!"

"Do you think perhaps we should seek the counsel—"

Darcy sighed with exasperation as she went to get her hat and gloves. "I know you think my better thoughts to be overcome by my vehemence, Priscilla, but my anger better enables me to do battle. Nathan may be a Barrington by blood, but he is a Sherwood in name and birth. And no pompous meddler, no matter his stature or wealth, will change that!"

Whirling on her heels, she stormed from the room with Priscilla struggling to keep pace. Encountering the page, Darcy requested that Mathilda's horse be brought around.

"Shall I come?" Priscilla asked.

Darcy shook her head. "You must stay by Nathan's side. If we must, we will leave London to a place where the Baron cannot find us."

"Nathan is with his tutor and Mama. Should I begin packing a portmanteau?"

"It may be advisable. I will bring word as soon as I have done with the Baron."

Darcy received one last parting embrace from her sister before she mounted the horse and directed it towards Grosvenor Square.

The audacity of the man! How dare he trifle with her family? Darcy fumed. Was this the Baron's way of exacting revenge upon her for having refused him?

Granted, he had been kind to pay for the new clothes, books, and tutor for Nathan. But they would have refused his benevolence had they known his true purpose! Never did a more odious man exist in all of England!

She did not know that the Baron would be home, of course. He could be out of town for all she knew, but her fury could not wait. If he had written the note to Priscilla himself and delivered it by courier, there was a chance that he had not left home yet for the day.

When she pulled up before Broadmoor House, the boldness with which she had spoken before Priscilla began to wane. In truth, there was little they could do if the Baron chose to exert his influence to take Nathan from them. Nothing but run away and begin their life anew. She had the fifty-thousand from Radcliff. It would more than suffice until she found another means of support.

But someone had to let the arrogant man understand that he could not do anything he damn well pleased just because he was a Barrington.

Forcing down her trepidation, Darcy mounted the steps of his residence resolutely. The butler greeted her once more with indifference and hesitantly allowed her passage.

"Is the Baron home?" Darcy inquired.

"He is, but, I believe, indisposed."

"I have an urgent matter which requires his attention."

The butler paused. "I will pass him that message, but perhaps you would wish to return at another time?"

"He will see me today," Darcy pronounced and sat down on a chair in the hallway. "I will wait until he is disposed."

"He may be busy the entire day."

"I have all day."

The butler stiffened. "If you will wait here, Miss Sherwood."

"I intend to."

When the butler returned, he indicated that his lordship would see her in his study. Darcy followed the butler, recalling the last time she had been here, also under unhappy circumstances.

"Miss Sherwood, my lord," the butler announced before leaving the two of them alone.

Radcliff, seated behind his writing desk, did not even lift his head but continued engrossed in whatever he was writing. Darcy waited for him to acknowledge her presence.

He didn't.

She pressed her lips together as she watched the quick movements of his pen. No one could excel at infuriating her more! He did not even look up when she stomped over and stood right in front of his desk.

Casting the letter he had written to Priscilla at him, her lips quivering with rage, Darcy declared, "Nathan is ours. You will never lay a hand upon him."

He finally looked up at her, and it was impossible to read his expression. The darkness of his eyes concealed his thoughts. "Are you not being rather presumptuous, Miss Sherwood?"

Presumptuous? His choice of words flabbergasted her. "Nathan has known no other family but us."

"He has a right to know the other half."

"There is no other half. For five years Edward has denied his son; he cannot expect to now dance into Nathan's life as if nothing had happened."

Radcliff folded the letter he had been writing with maddening calm. "Nathan will not be raised as Edward's son; he will be in my custody and raised, nonetheless, as a Barrington."

"Your custody?" Darcy flamed. "Nathan is not your responsibility. If this is a means of assuaging your guilt for the part that you played—"

"Regardless of my motivations, is it not in the best interest of

Nathan to be given all the privileges that come with his heritage?"

"It is not in his interest to be taken away from his mother!"

"Neither you nor your sister would be barred from visiting Nathan now and then."

Darcy's eyes widened. She and Priscilla would be relegated to 'visits'? 'Now and then'?

"You contemptible overbearing bastard," Darcy cried. How she hated the man! Hated how he sat there without the slightest emotion while she was twisted with fury and fear.

"I appreciate your sentiments of me, but I hardly think they persuade your case."

"What is it you want?" Darcy seethed. "Is it the money you gave me in exchange for the deed to Brayten? I would give anything to never see or hear the name of Barrington again!"

"Anything?" He raised an eyebrow.

"Anything," Darcy spat.

He crossed one leg over the other and considered the matter while Darcy wondered how best to wring the man's neck.

"I will relinquish my pursuit to obtain Nathan," he announced.

Darcy perked up. Had she heard correctly?

"On two conditions," Radcliff continued, rising to his feet. He stood before her. It was all she could do to stand her ground and not be overpowered by his aura.

"What conditions?" she asked. He was so close she could smell him, the scent alone awakening all her raw animal senses.

He looked down at her and this time she saw in his eyes a hunger that a predator might have when beholding its prey.

"That you submit to me. Here. Now."

Her knees began to shake, and she could barely swallow. "Here?"

"And now."

By the hard set of his jaw, Darcy could see that he was not jesting. Why was he doing this? Part of her wanted to run. Part of her was thrilled that he wanted her still.

"You give your word that you will not attempt to take Nathan from us?" she asked, wondering where her towering rage had disappeared to all of a sudden.

"My word. In writing if you wish."

She trusted him. He was insufferable but his integrity was in tact.

"Very well," Darcy surrendered, wondering how she was going to explain it all to her sister.

Holding her immobile with the strength of his gaze, he gently pulled at the ribbon of her bonnet until it came undone. Darcy closed her eyes as he removed her bonnet and tossed it aside. He might as well have torn her entire dress away—she felt naked before him. Would he kiss her now?

But Radcliff stepped away. She felt as if chains had been lifted from her, but the absence of his closeness was both liberating and poignant. She watched him as he went back to his writing desk and sat down. Was the heat in his eyes from anger? Did he want to make her pay for rejecting him?

"Take off your dress," he ordered.

"I cannot reach the pins in back," Darcy responded with defiance.

"Then you must tear the dress from your body."

Remembering the time he had commanded her to tear her shift, Darcy felt an old familiar warmth begin to fan from her loins.

"But..." Darcy stalled, studying her dress to see if there was a way it could be easily reassembled after being torn. Did he mean to provide her with another dress? Somehow she doubted it for there were no signs of sympathy in his eyes.

"I am waiting, Miss Sherwood."

"Perhaps you could assist with the pins, sir—my lord?" she offered.

A smile tugged at the corner of his mouth. "Perhaps. But that is not what I suggested."

Darcy frowned. She would have to reconcile herself to purchasing a new morning dress. Unhappily, she grasped the hem of the gown and stretched it between her two hands. It took a number of attempts, but the fabric eventually gave way. As the sound of her gown ripping filled the air, Darcy vacillated between feeling enraged and aroused.

She hated him. Hated him for blackmailing her into submission—for the second time. But most of all, she hated him for making her submission feel so *good*.

"Well done," he commended when she had slipped her arms free of the gown. "Now remove the petticoats and stays."

Fortunately her stays fastened in front. It and the petticoats fell to the ground around her feet.

"And the shift—I want it torn."

"It's the one you bought," Darcy said hotly. Despite her lack of clothing, she felt warm from head to toe.

"Yes, I recognize it. Tear it."

"But what will I wear when I leave?" Darcy asked in a panic.

"That is your dilemma, Miss Sherwood... You could simply leave in the buff."

Darcy emitted a cry, then glared at him. His lack of concern enraged her. This was retaliation. He meant to settle the score by requiring not just her submission but her complete humiliation as well. If it weren't for Nathan, she would have whirled on her heels and left, never mind the dampness that had begun forming between her legs.

As if reading her mind, he said, "The love you bear your nephew is commendable."

"Well you know anything of love!" Darcy snapped. "You are a heartless and callous lout."

"The shift, Miss Sherwood."

Stifling a scream, Darcy ripped the thin cotton garment as if it were a metaphor for how she felt about him. She now stood before him without a shred of clothing, and though her nakedness was nothing new to him, she felt the need to cover her bosom and groin.

"Such modesty does not become you, my dear," Radcliff noted with a sardonic grin. "Turn around."

Darcy did as she was told, the lack of emotion in his voice making her feel as if she were a simply a slab of beef that he was inspecting. She watched him as he appraised her, his gaze touching upon every inch of her body. The shadow beneath her breasts. The subtle swell of her belly.

"Touch your breasts for me," he directed, and for the first time Darcy thought she detected a tremor in his voice. "With both hands."

She reached up and cradled one globe in each hand.

"Fondle them," he clarified.

She kneaded her breasts, first slowly and lightly, then harder and faster as she felt sensations rippling from her breasts down to her belly. She pinched both her nipples and softly groaned.

"Stop," he ordered brusquely and rose to his feet.

She continued to dig her fingers into her flesh and pushed the orbs together.

"Stop," he repeated and dashed her hands from her breasts.

She felt a wave of disappointment.

"Your ability to follow orders is wanting, Miss Sherwood," he commented as he walked around her like a hawk circling its prey. "Such defiance must be addressed. Stand against the table with your feet apart."

He leaned her forward onto his desk and spread her legs so that her buttocks were more than adequately exposed for him.

"That," he said after he delivered the first smack to her derrière, "is for your hesitation. This for your defiance."

Darcy nearly flew over the writing desk with the second slap.

"And your impudence...."

Her knees shook with the force of the third and fourth strikes. Her arse burned with the spanking, but a smoldering ache was building between her legs.

"Do not question me again, Miss Sherwood," Radcliff told her and added another whack for good measure.

He reached beneath her to discover her wetness had begun to slide down her thigh. Darcy suppressed a whimper.

He instructed her to lie across the writing table on her back and reached down to the floor and picked up the shift, which he tore in twain. With each half, he tied her legs to the legs of the table so that the softest parts of her flesh were exposed to view. With her dress, he bound her wrists together and pulled her arms over her head, securing them to the remaining two legs of the table.

The damn thing—the table and the manner in which she was stretched across it—was exceedingly uncomfortable. Silently, Darcy cursed Radcliff and promised herself she would make him pay for this.

His gaze traveled the length of her body from her toes to the elbows on either side of her head. She saw a facial muscle twitch along his jaw. He ran a hand languidly from her knee and up her thigh. Darcy caught her breath when his fingers grazed her belly button and cupped a breast. She shivered when his thumb passed over her nipple. She hoped he would touch her again. She was sure to spend quick if he did.

But to her dismay, he stepped away, saying as he surveyed her, "Most delectable, but I have at present an appointment to keep."

Darcy felt the air sucked from her. She opened her eyes and looked at him as if through a haze. Had she heard him correctly? But then she watched in horror as he put on his gloves.

"Oh, please…" she whispered through parched lips.

He raised an eyebrow. He was going to make her beg, she realized. So be it. She needed to spend as if her life depended upon it.

"Please…take me," she whimpered.

"Why?"

The question went screaming through her mind. She was going to go mad if he didn't make her come soon.

"Because I desire it…because you have made me desire it…"

"How much?"

"I crave it immensely…desperately…" she said through her blurred thoughts. "No one makes me feel as you do."

"No one?"

"No one," she confirmed. "No one can bring such delight…my body longs for your touch…"

"Is it mine to do as I please?"

"Yes, yes, my body is yours. Yours alone. Radcliff … take me now."

He smiled and planted a tender kiss upon her brow. Grabbing the letter he had been writing earlier, he donned his hat and said, "In due time, my love."

Her eyes widened in panic. She gave him a wild look. He was not going to leave her bound to the writing table?

"Ring for my servants if you require anything," he offered before closing the door after him.

Her desire ached with emptiness, and she attempted to will herself to spend. He had left her on the worst precipice she had ever known. Darcy struggled against her bindings. Good God, what if a servant walked in? She struggled harder.

The minutes dragged on. But all she could do was wait.

=

IT HAD KILLED HIM TO leave her there, her quivering body tied to his writing table. Radcliff wanted nothing more than to help her achieve the greatest ecstasy her body could know. But it was true that he had an appointment.

She would hate him for this. But it was worth it to hear her utter her desire. *Yes, yes, my body is yours. Yours alone.*

She would not believe him if he told her that he suffered with her. His arousal had strained against him from the moment she attempted to tear her dress. If it could speak, it would have howled in rage against him for not allowing it to sink into her wetness. It had taken every ounce of restraint when he had witnessed that clear honey glistening down the length of her and onto the surface of the writing table.

But she would understand now that she was his and could only be his. And he knew now, more than ever, that he was hers and could only be hers.

"Miss Sherwood's horse is still here," his perplexed butler explained to Radcliff upon his return.

"Yes, I know," Radcliff said briskly as he tossed his hat and gloves to the man. He could wait no longer. He had to have her.

He opened the door to his study and was relieved and guilt-ridden to see her still tied to his writing table. She was struggling against her bindings liked a caged animal. Hoping he had not tied her bonds too tightly, he silently promised her that he would make it up to her—for the rest of his life. He sauntered over to inspect her.

She was wetter than ever.

Thank God, Radcliff thought. His assumption had been correct. When he met her eyes, which were casting daggers at him, he gave her his best devilish grin. Still defiant. And he would have it no other way with Darcy Sherwood.

"I know you, Radcliff," Pinkerton had told him, "need someone as bloody cocky as yourself."

She was perfect for him, Radcliff concluded as he stared at her beautiful bound body. In wit, passion, honesty, and flesh, his match—and better. It was time to bring her to the rapture she deserved.

He reached between her legs and stroked her. Her body responded like a well-tuned instrument. She had been hanging on the edge of spending for so long that it did not take her long to climax. Spasms erupted throughout her body. Her body would have arched off the table if not for her bonds.

Before she completely recovered from her orgasm, Radcliff undid her bonds and flipped her over onto her stomach. With her breasts flattened by the desk and her arse hanging deliciously off the edge of the table, he drew out his length and pushed it into her. Having been deprived of her for so long, it felt as if he were entering her for the very first time.

It felt sublime.

After only a few well drawn thrusts, he had Darcy riding her second orgasm. His orgasm came with a blinding fury. His thighs shook as he pumped himself into her once, twice, thrice. He felt like collapsing on top of her, but he knew she must have been sore from being tied to the writing table. Collecting her body in his arms, he carried her over to the sofa. She breathed what sounded like a contented sigh and leaned her head against him.

This, too, felt sublime.

He massaged her arms and kissed her eyelashes. He murmured into her hair, "This is merely the beginning, my dearest Darcy."

She tensed and seemed to awaken from her daze. "Your condition was that I submit to you here and now. The 'now' has passed, my lord."

"If you recall I had two conditions."

"Two conditions?" she echoed apprehensively. "What is the second?"

"That you give your hand to me in matrimony."

At first she only blinked, then she looked at him as if he were playing a cruel jest upon her.

"I want you for my own, Miss Sherwood," Radcliff explained.

"But…what of being your mistress?"

"You refused me."

Still confused, Darcy asked, "But you think I would accept an offer of marriage instead?"

"Well, I hadn't planned on it being an offer," Radcliff said. "My appointment, you see, was to secure the minister and leave notice with *The Times*. The banns will be read this Sunday."

Her eyes widened. Radcliff could not tell if she was appalled or impressed.

"Do you mean to refuse me a second time?" he asked when she had not spoken.

"What of Nathan?"

"He, your sister, and your stepmother will be provided for. If they choose to live in London, I will find them a townhome. If they prefer the country, there is my primary seat or my secondary estate near Brighton."

"You won't take Nathan from Priscilla then?"

The relief and hope in her voice made him feel like a rotten cad. He responded brusquely, "Of course not, though I had to do something to command your attention—and force your hand."

She shook her head. "You are the most arrogant and abominable man."

"So you've said."

"And if I were to decline?"

Radcliff clenched his jaw, and his features darkened. "It is not an option. Do you realize that you could be with child? I will *not* have another bastard to the Barrington name."

Her eyes widened but she looked away quickly—too quickly.

"Good God," Radcliff exhaled. He grabbed her by the shoulders and turned her to him. "*Are* you with child?"

She looked at him in protest, but no words came.

"That settles the matter then," he said grimly. "Thank God I set an early wedding date."

Was that relief lighting her face? Happiness? Then horror filled her eyes as she uttered, "I would be Mrs. Barrington!"

Radcliff could not resist a half smile. "Yes, the fourth Baroness Broadmoor."

"But why?"

"You disappoint me, Miss Sherwood. I took you for a clever woman, but it would seem obvious, even to the dumb, that I adore you. I adore you body and soul. I want to be the only man to command pleasure from you. I want to bring you joy in all its forms from the moment the sun rises to the moment the moon sets. And I wish it for the rest of my life."

He could see tears welling in her eyes. It was nearly his undoing.

"And I believe," he continued, "that you bear some affection for me as well."

"A little," she acknowledge with a wry smile.

He kissed the tear that slid down the side of her face before capturing her mouth was his. Unlike the fierce kisses of desire, this one was tender and bespoke the love he felt for her.

"Darling Darcy," he murmured into her hair and pulled her close. The *ton* be damned for nothing could make him feel this contented, this complete, as she.

"I have a condition of my own, Baron," said Darcy as she pulled away to look up at him.

"Indeed?"

Her eyes gleamed with mischief at him. "You must submit to *me* on our wedding night."

Radcliff considered for a moment. "Very well, Baroness, and you will be mine through the honeymoon."

Darcy shook her head. "I don't think I shall ever become accustomed to being addressed as a Baroness. Priscilla would...Priscilla will wonder what has become of me! I should speak with her at once—oh! My *clothing!*"

Radcliff offered her his coat. "You shall pen a letter to your sister, and I will have my servant deliver it post-haste. As for the dress, one of my maids can sew it well enough for you to depart in it."

Flushing, she accepted the coat. The blush in her cheeks made her look angelic. Radcliff stared at her. How was it possible that she could look so damned attractive even in his clothing?

"It will take some time to mend the dress. What are we to do till then?" she inquired.

"I would like to ravish you once or twice more," Radcliff responded as he adjusted his cock, "though I will require a brief respite. What does my lady recommend to pass the time?"

She gave him a smile that thrilled him to no end.

"Have you a deck a cards, my lord?"

THE END

ABOUT GEORGETTE BROWN

Georgette Brown is the "nice" alter-ego
to Em Brown's "naughtiness."

Her current works include:

PRIDE, PREJUDICE & PLEASURE
THAT WICKED HARLOT
AN INDECENT WAGER

DON'T FORGET

You can receive a FREE BOOK from

Georgette Brown:

http://dl.bookfunnel.com/62lpwgvwxh

AN INDECENT WAGER

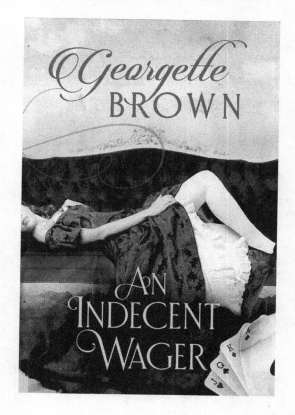

CPSIA information can be obtained
at www.ICGtesting.com
Printed in the USA
BVHW032255300920
590057BV00001B/61

9 781942 822219